Ganja Tales II

Second Edition

Updated edition published in 2022 by
The Writing Dog LLC
Omaha, NE

Printed and distributed by Ingram Spark
and Lightning Source

ISBN: 978-0-9701140-4-4

Ganja Tales originally published in 2000 by
The Pugh Press, Omaha, NE
Ganja Tales -2nd edition published in 2019 by
Tablo Publishing

Ganja Tales II

Second Edition

by Craig Pugh

For Ian, a fine son and best friend.

And to all the brothers and sisters who languish in jail
for smoking the herb. Our prayers are with you.

Table of Contents

Reefer Madness

A person does strange things when no one's watching.

The marijuana sat on a white pedestal in the middle of the room. Looked like a nice ounce or so of fat kind buds. But the people lounging about the sofas and chairs, drinking wine and smoking cigarettes were ignoring the green goodies.

Mike couldn't figure out why. And he so wanted to get high.

To make matters worse, in this dream he didn't have a lighter, papers or pipe. So he couldn't shout: "Look everybody -- some wacky weed! Let's load a bowl and find out if it's any good."

He was asleep, then awake; asleep, awake; then felt himself come back to reality as tires squealed outside his apartment. Waiting for his eyes to open and his rational mind to work, it hit him: Marijuana was in the apartment. He couldn't get to it -- didn't know where it was, in fact. He only knew the buds were somewhere nearby. His roommate had hidden them. Where though?

Funny, just like in his dream. The stuff was there; he just couldn't get to it. Then his brain went soft as his dream-river returned, rolling over him again, pulling him under.

The marijuana was the reason he'd passed out. Well, and Marcy. Marcy appeared out of the blue just a few hours ago with the weed, a full half-pound. She and Sean, his roommate, had known each other since second grade. She moved to Dallas with her mother last year and knew plenty of dealers down there now.

When Marcy broke out the weed she explained how there was a lot more marijuana in Dallas, and all Sean needed to do was help her sell this half-pound (a mere 8-ounces for a weed-starved city!) and they could drive back to Texas where, she was sure, with a couple hundred bucks down, she could get a few pounds of reefer fronted to her by her mom's biker friends.

Mike had listened to them talking it over as they examined the buds and got thoroughly wasted. The Texas nugs were good commercial weed, light-green, copper-blond highlights.

Listening to Sean and Marcy making plans, Mike felt left out although he wouldn't have gone with them had they asked. Not only was he in school, but he wasn't one to just take off like that. He liked more continuity in his life.

And he woke again, a bag of skin and bones. A couple gallons of blood. Trying to get it all working.

Okay brain. Turn yourself on. Think.

Sean and Marcy were out getting the oil changed on her Camaro. Marcy . . . always grinning in spite of having survived a lousy childhood. Numerous DWIs, possession-under-an-ounce. Getting knocked around by jerk boyfriends on a regular basis. Her devil-may-care attitude complemented her tight blue jeans and cowgirl boots, and she tore through life in her red Camaro like she was leading the barrel-racers at the county rodeo.

Mike got out of bed and found himself pausing in front of Sean's closed bedroom door. Then his hand was on the knob and he knew, of course, that he was by himself in the apartment . . .

The bedroom looked like the same mess it was when they'd left it after smoking earlier. The only thing missing was the weed. Mike walked over to Sean's desk, stood on the chair and looked along the top bookshelf. He knew from experience Sean sometimes kept his stash there. Maybe he'd left something from the half-pound that Mike could pinch. That would be nice. Actually, Mike was surprised they hadn't left him something to get by on until they returned. They had eight ounces. One would hardly miss a nug from a stash like that!

He opened the cabinet doors and surveyed the contents. No weed. He pulled the drawers out, looked behind them. Nothing again. Then he caught himself. It flashed in his mind that Sean was standing in the door behind him, waiting to say "What are you doing going through my things!?"

Suddenly feeling embarrassed, Mike left the bedroom and headed for the ice-cream in the kitchen. He ate a spoon full and looked at the two robins in the crabapple tree outside his kitchen window, gathering straw for their nest.

Thunder rumbled out west on the edge of the prairie and the air smelled like rain coming. He needed to go shopping, and he needed to study for a biology test next week. But it was Saturday and his thoughts drifted to Sean and Marcy. Earlier, when they had smoked out, Mike offered to chip in a couple hundred on their deal, but they fell quiet when he suggested it. Then Sean said: "I got it Bro. But we'll set you up – don't worry."

Then Mike knew Sean and Marcy were going to make big bucks off the deal and he was going to be left out in the cold.

Fine, he thought. *Whatever.* Still, they should have left him something.

He finished the ice-cream while standing at the window, and realized he just ate the whole pint. This made him happy. About time he ate something before Sean got to it! Sean wasn't shy about taking anything from the fridge--mainly the beer, sodas and ice-cream--whenever he wanted to. Of course, in spite of promises to pay Mike back, Sean never did.

He then thought that Sean could have stashed the weed in the kitchen cabinets. It could in fact be inches from his face. So he looked: among the tea and rice boxes on the shelf above the stove; in the tall shelves to the right of it where they kept the canned goods; below, down by the pots and pans; and finally, in the space under the sink. Nada. Nothing.

Christ, where were those buds?

He called Sean's cellular. They were still waiting, probably at least another hour. "Hang on," Sean said. "We'll get some beers on the way home and start partying as soon as we get there."

"Where you at?" Mike asked. "It doesn't sound like you're at a garage." He heard a juke box pumping rap beats in the background.

"We're not, dude. We got a pitcher and a pizza and we're waiting for the car," he laughed, and hung up.

That bastard! Mike thought. *Always having a good time and leaving me out.* Deep down he knew that he took life more seriously than Sean did -- wanted more from it, and therefore couldn't treat it with the same recklessness Sean did.

Still, Sean owed him. Who paid for the cable subscription? Mike did. Plus, he was always loaning Sean his car or driving him somewhere because Sean was too lazy to fix his own car and couldn't keep it running anyway because he spent all his money on drugs. Sean was always, therefore, broke and high, which is probably why he mooched cigarettes shamelessly from Mike.

Mike got mad just thinking about it. For everything he'd done, not to be cut-in on Marcy's deal just plain pissed him off. It seemed pretty evident to him that Sean was taking advantage of him. *So what*, he told himself. *Don't get attached.*

On the way back to his room, Mike paused at Sean's door, staring at the dirty beige carpet beneath his feet, thinking about how he wouldn't like someone going through his room. He stood a full minute, debating, hand on the doorknob; but then, ever so slowly, opened it and stared into the bedroom.

Once he took that first step inside, Mike felt like he had burst out of a jungle into a clearing. He crouched, animal-like, nostrils flaring. *Smell the marijuana.* He concentrated, trying to imagine a fruity green aroma emanating from some place in the room. Nothing.

Okay, what the hell. *Think. Where would you hide a half-pound of fat Texas nugs?* Aha! The ol' laundry basket trick. He'd used that one himself before. In Sean's closet he pulled all the laundry from the hamper, his heart racing. *Half-pound, half-pound, come on half-pound!* Man was he going to get stoned. He felt a lump toward the bottom, pulled it up and -- a bundled-up shirt.

Hmm. The top shelf. Mike got a chair, stood on it, began opening the various games: Monopoly. Life. Checkers. Then the puzzles: London Bridge, Mickey Mouse, a forest scene. Each one opened and examined. Nothing, although the dust triggered his sinus, making him sneeze repeatedly. Next shelf down were the sweaters; then all the shirt and pants. He patted down all the pockets. Nothing. How about inside all the shoes and boots on the closet floor? Nope. Okay, not in the closet? No big deal. Keep looking.

The weed's probably in Sean's dresser drawers. Five drawers, underwear on top and old jeans on the bottom: He went through them quickly, skimming his hand underneath the contents of each one. In the bottom drawer, underneath a stack of faded jeans, a paperback: "Memoirs of an English Maid." Jesus, he muttered, opening the book to a random page:

"Oh master, no," I begged him desperately as he undressed in front of me. Since I was a virgin I had of course never seen a man, I assure you, yet I was defenseless. I writhed in the iron cuffs biting at my wrists and ankles, and strained to close my legs against the chains that had them pulled so far apart. The

shame, sir, the shame! Lord Dimmsley snorted drunkenly and let out a long, evil laugh that spoke of many years of wine and debauchery. He lurched toward my exposed womanhood, for I lay naked upon the table, my embarrassment spreading in a red glow across my Christian face and breasts. And then I screamed . . .

Mike shut the book. *Wow*, he thought. He had no idea. He was rearranging the drawer to its original condition when he also discovered a Hustler magazine. He let out a low whistle. Dang, that Sean was a busy guy. Still, no nugs. He looked at the bookshelf against the wall. He swung his hand behind the paperbacks, but no luck. Just a bunch of dust and a sharp prick from a stray pin. Sonofabitch! he cursed, pinching his fingertip and watching a fat splot of blood well up.

He felt the anger rising in himself when he washed his hands in the bathroom, felt it rise quickly and flush his face. He was upset at himself for all of this. He hadn't meant to take the search so far that it filled his mind and thoughts and drove him to compromise his principles like this. He certainly didn't want to think of himself as someone who was so addicted that he would search his roommate's possessions for buds. But if he looked at the facts, here he was, violating Sean's privacy.

And yet, drying his hands, Mike knew he wasn't going to walk away from the search. Not now. No, a brush fire running hot and wild was spreading rapidly inside him, and he knew only one way to put it out. He had to find the weed.

Maybe Sean stashed the dope right under his nose. He dropped to his knees and looked under the sink behind the toilet paper, combs, brushes and bottles of old shampoo. Nada. Okay, the stuff could be in the living room. He went out and looked behind the sofa against the wall. Nope. All right. The coffee table in front of the couch. He opened the two doors, pulled out all the videos. *No cigar buddy, no cigar.* The closet? Check behind the vacuum cleaner. No again. The pockets on the coats and jackets; but again, nothing. "Shit!" he exclaimed, clenching his fists. His blood-pressure skyrocketed.

He looked in the roll-top desk against the wall, practically ripping the six drawers out of their sockets. *What in the holy hell does a guy have to do to get high around here?* he wondered. Paper clips, notes, pencils, bills -- all tumbled onto the floor. Everything, in fact, but the marijuana. It took Mike the better part of half-an-hour to painstakingly put all the knick-knacks back in original order, drawer by drawer, before he could sit down at the kitchen table and take a shot of vodka to calm his nerves down. He tried -- he really tried -- sitting there, shaking, spinning in a centrifuge of pure white rage. He tried to simmer down.

He picked up the vodka bottle and, hell, took a slug, not a sip, then returned to Sean's bedroom, frustrated yet recharged for the search. A man with a mission: find the dope. Hey, he reasoned, it wasn't his fault he was going through his buddy's things. His "buddy" should have left him a nug to begin with, then Mike wouldn't be in this position. Anyway, Sean would do the same thing to him, the conniving bastard. Why, he ripped Mike off every day!

He searched underneath the cushion on the easy chair, then stared at the old rocker. A person could lift it from the front and push it back and see a perfect hiding place in its hollow frame. He lifted it and looked. Nothing.

Come on buddy, he told himself. *Your time's running out*! He figured he'd been searching at least an hour now, maybe longer. Time he could've spent doing something constructive. But no . . . not him. What was the friggin' difficulty? You'd think half a pound of marijuana would be easy enough to find in a little two-bedroom apartment. He could imagine those fat juicy nugs, how they would taste and smell. Most of all, how they would get him high. Holy Christ how he wanted to find them! *Come on baby, come to papa.*

He ripped Sean's mattress off. He'd searched everywhere else he could think of. Time to find some weed and get high brother!

Mike heaved the mattress against the wall and the first thing that caught his eye was a packet of wax paper on the box springs. *What the hell?* He carefully opened it, placed his fingertip against the white crystals and then put it in his mouth. *Well I'll be damned*, he thought. *Sean's got a frikken eight ball of coke!* Also on the mattress, a stack of twenties. Mike counted them. Three-hundred dollars! "You bastard," he said out loud. Sean had owed him $300 for months now. No wonder he'd delayed in repaying him. He was shoving coke up his nose!

Mike didn't do chemicals or powder. He just smoked loco weed. That's all he wanted, some moon cabbage, a little bit of reefer madness. Was that asking too much? Where in the hell were the buds? He was not only running out of places to search, he was also running out of time. Surely they'd be back any minute. He fast-walked to the kitchen window. From there he could see who came in the building. No red Camaro. *Hurry! Find the marijuana!*

He returned to Sean's room, lifted the box springs and slammed it against the wall. Well, how 'bout that, a Smith & Wesson 9mm. Christ! He didn't know Sean had a gun. Sean was crazy, especially when he was drunk, which was often. It scared Mike knowing Sean had a pistol. Why hadn't he told anyone? And an envelope, a letter to Sean from his mother. The postmark was five years old. Why would Sean keep a letter five years old? Mike took it out and began reading it.

My Dearest Sean,
I have to tell you this because you have a right to know who your real father is . . .

Oh my God, Mike thought. *Sean's dad isn't his real dad? What was that all about?* Then a big wave of guilt hit him. He didn't want to know all this stuff, didn't want to pry into things he had no business prying into. All he wanted was a buzz on the 420! But that wasn't going to happen; he knew that now. He had simply run out of places to look. No magic-act rabbits squirming out of any hats today. He stopped reading the letter and put it back in the envelope, noticed his hand was shaking. *Goddamn nerves!*

His head was a boulder he held between his hands now, shaking it slowly back and forth, clenching his eyes shut and moaning "No . . ." He couldn't stop his energy from seething and boiling up into the colors of a bruise: black, purple, crimson tinged with yellow, until finally he exploded in a nuclear mushroom cloud of rage and frustration. One detonation took out the right side of his brain, the other one the left.

Somehow in the middle of that rage-violence he heard the muffled whump of car doors closing, and he ran to the window in time to see Sean chasing Marcy to the stairwell door, grabbing her, swaying drunkenly. Her laughing.

Mike raced for the living room sofa and flopped down, pretending to be asleep, praying he'd put everything back in place in all the rooms. Calm down, he thought. Just calm down. Footsteps and giggles floating up the stairwell, the duo of fun-loving drug dealers inside, Sean standing by the couch.

"Hey dude, what's up? Taking a nap on us?"

Mike blinked and acted sleepy. Sean tossed him a beer and Mike caught the cold can just before it thudded into his chest. Sean went in the kitchen to put the beer in the fridge, and when he returned he held the marijuana.

"You okay?" he asked. "You look like shit. I thought you'd be tearing the place apart searching for this," and he tossed Mike the half pound, slightly chilled from being in the fridge.

"Geez," Mike replied. "Give me some credit. You think I'd rip off my homey? I've just been lying here trying to get rid of a headache."

Bright Lights And Live Wires

*If ever there was a 420 Hall of Fame,
Eddie would be in it.*

You're staring at the western sky on the night I'm describing, watching the sun sink in a glorious melting sprawl of red, purple and orange, and you're thinking: *You know, life can be pretty good.*

And if you're lucky like I was you have a friend to drink a pint with and smoke a joint with, too; and you're sitting at an outside table like one at Joe's Brew House in Denver just as Mark and I were doing that night.

Mark fished a joint from his pocket and slowly spun it around with his fingertips, smoothing it for proper smoking while the sun set itself in darkness. Then click! Mark lit the joint and at the moment the flame sprang to life it lit up the face of an old fellow sitting behind us against the wall. Sitting there all by himself he was. Mark saw him before I did.

"Dude!" Mark exclaimed. "You scared the shit out of me! Where'd you come from?"

I turned and saw a thin man about fifty-five years old with long, wavy-blond gray hair brushed back over a worrisome-looking face. He was plainly dressed like the rest of us in blue jeans, tennis shoes and T-shirts but stood out in that his skin was ghostly pale like that of a person who hadn't seen sunlight in years.

Or perhaps he was just recovering from an illness.

His high cheekbones, deep eye sockets and wiry eyebrows along with a fine, prominent nose gave him the look of a wise old bird – an owl or an eagle, I suppose. And I never thought of blue as a painful color until I found myself staring into his eyes burning like two dark sapphires in his white face.

He spoke then through a slight grin. "Sorry gents. Didn't mean to alarm you. Slipped in quietly, I reckon."

And we heard that his voice was one of *those* voices: whiskey-soaked, barrel-aged; tinged with grief, touched by sadness. It was a great voice.

And I forget which came first – the thunder or the wind – but after he spoke a huge thunder-boomer belched in the distance and came scudding down Larimore Street in a series of ground-shaking rumbles, followed by an icy breeze that roared like a waterfall flying in off the Rockies. Some people went inside and those who stayed turned up collars or pulled hoods over heads.

"What the hell!" Mark said, hitting the joint a few times and taking a righteous quaff of his hoppy ale. I smoked and found myself looking over at that curious fellow now looking back at me with his smoldering blue eyes.

"Well, you might as well join us if you wish," I said to him. "I hate to see a man drinking alone."

His glass was near-empty and we had a fresh pitcher so I pointed to it and added: "We may need some help with this."

He came over and sat, saying "Thanks, guys."

I was glad. Nothing makes a fair mood go foul faster than a person who rejects your good will overtures.

And I missed it at the time but, looking back, wasn't it peculiar that when he sat down with us the wind disappeared and the thunder with it?

"I didn't mean to stare," he said, "but it's just so hard for me to comprehend you guys sitting out here smoking bud and drinking brews."

"Why what do you mean?" I asked, filling his glass with beer. "It's always been this way."

He sat straight up and his blue eyes turned violet-black. "Oh no it hasn't!" he nearly shouted.

I'm telling you, that dude put a chill in my veins. You could just tell something dark had got ahold of him.

So I thought a minute about what he'd said, and I replied: "Of course, my parents have told me of the times when marijuana was illegal."

"You bet it was," the stranger said. "And all the stuff that came with it. So there was nothing, even lights. It's not like you drove to the store and bought a thousand-watt sodium or halide."

"Weird," Mark said. "You need a good light to grow good weed."

The stranger shook his head in agreement. "Indeed you do," he said.

We sipped our beers and the glowing tip of the joint bobbed around to each us as we smoked in silence and happiness, and the camaraderie of just being there. The stranger said how good the marijuana was and we sat another minute before I asked: "Well, did you grow weed or what?"

He smiled. "Back in the day, me and my buddy had a bullshit growing room with four plants under fluorescent tubes."

Mark and I looked at each other. I grimaced and he chuckled.

"Sorry," I said. "It's just that; well, by today's standards you had a three G platform."

"Oh I know," he said. "But this was a long time ago and I lived in a Republican state where the prisons were overcrowded and you could go to jail at the drop of a hat."

"I am grateful I was born in Colorado," Mark replied.

"Me, too!" I added, then asked the stranger where he was from.

"Military brat," he said. "Then twelve year's active-duty myself. So I'm from nowhere."

I asked him where he was born and he said Greeley and I replied Weld County kid, huh?

He said he wished they hadn't moved when he was two years old so he could remember something about Colorado, but he didn't.

"You live here now?" Mark asked.

"Just got here. We'll see."

I told him: "Welcome back to Colorado, friend," and he nodded appreciation while I poured more beer into his glass. I'm telling you there was something curious about that guy. So I asked him if he ever did score a decent growing light and he said sorta and I said what's 'sorta' mean?

He closed his eyes and shook his head back and forth slowly and his lips drew inward, as if tasting a bitter memory. "Well," he finally said. "If you fellas got a minute I'll tell you a good old-fashioned marijuana story."

I looked at Mark who shrugged and said: "I ain't going anywhere."

Neither was I. The moon was rising in the sky. Pretty girls were walking by. Me? Content, my friend. Very content. The joint went round a time or two and as we sat and drank our brews we saw the old fellow trying to begin his story. He stared off long and hard into space until finally he got to a place in his head where the movie camera started playing some of it for him.

"Go back thirty-five years ago, before you guys were born," he said, "to Omaha, Nebraska. I was putting up roof with Eddie. He was foreman of the crew and my roommate."

Mark interrupted. "I only ever heard of people leaving Nebraska -- not going there."

"And for good reason," the stranger replied, adding: "Don't ever catch me in Nebraska again, or up on a roof. That is some hot damn work."

But there he was, he said, in Omaha with Eddie the roofer. Eddie was a daredevil. He rode a loud and noisy dirt bike on city streets, skydived on weekends and drove an old green Chrysler with the words NO FEAR emblazoned in a raw slash across the trunk. He wasn't the brightest bulb. He just had a lot of guts, a bad muffler and a leaky damn water pump.

"Man, that guy was always up to something. And everything he did was held together by chewing gum, baling wire and duct tape," the stranger said.

Then he chuckled.

"But by God -- never a dull moment! Ready Eddie – that's what we called him."

Mark pulled out another joint and fired it up. "So what happened to ol' Eddie?" he asked.

The stranger took a long, steady pull from it and exhaled slowly, enjoying the smoke.

"That's some really nice weed, guys," he said. "I appreciate it."

He was a friendly sort and we sure didn't mind talking with him as we were now anxious to hear his story.

Well, he says, Eddie had his eye on a thousand-watt halide high on a pole lighting up Fire Station No. 5 on the western edge of town. That light shined like the sun out there in the wee hours of the morning – lit up the whole damn parking lot. How he was ever going to shimmy up that pole and get the light down after he disabled it was beyond me. You have to understand the times, he continued. If you wanted to grow, you had to go out and get a light by hook or by crook.

"I had friends who snagged all four of the thousand-watters lighting the university bell tower," he laughed. "University cops chased them all the way off campus. We thought that was cool as shit. Put the whole damn bell tower in darkness. Screw that college.

Took all my money to get a degree and I couldn't find a job."

I pondered that this Eddie guy was one of those original growers from back in the day that you hear about every so often. How crazy was that? I topped our glasses off and leaned forward. "So," I asked. "Did you and Eddie get that light?"

"Goddamnit!" he exclaimed. "I told Eddie not to do it. But he wanted that light so badly. He'd say 'Just think of the size buds we could grow! Buds the size of your fist!' He had a point. I just didn't know anything about electricity. Eddie said he did. He said he had it all worked out. He said he would buy a pair of rubber gloves and the biggest loppers he could find and go out all ninja-style one night and cut that light down. That was Eddie. He was always in it to win it and down for a good caper."

Mark said: "Uh-oh. That doesn't sound too good."

"No," the stranger replied. "It wasn't. But back then you were either a ganja guerilla or not. And we were down for it. We considered ourselves part of the 420 resistance."

"Wow," I said.

"Yep," the stranger continued. "Times were sure different. And Eddie . . . he just had to have that light. That thousand-watter was his crack cocaine, the itch he had to scratch."

He leaned forward and took a long drink of beer from his glass. "Jeez they make good beer nowadays!" he exclaimed, a statement that made me wonder where he'd been. I filled his glass back up.

He then told us how Eddie started researching how a typical municipal electrical grid worked. Eddie was already somewhat of an electrician and he could damn sure throw up a roof in a hurry. Handy, that's what he was. Then one night after supper out of the blue Eddie says he's gonna try and get the light tomorrow night.

"And I says to him: Eddie, let's *look at it* tomorrow night. We'll go down and you show me what you wanna do and we'll talk about the plan. You're gonna need my help, right?"

Eddie says yes, of course dude.

"So we go down the next night close to midnight. We drive back and forth on the street and we're casing the place out. We get back to the house and talk about what we just saw and Eddie shows me his ingress and egress route.

"Eddie," I says. "I'm worried. You'll have to cross an open field to get to the light. You'll be very visible."

Of course he told me not to be a pussy and balls out is the only way to go.

Then he said tomorrow night was the night and it rolled around like it always does and Eddie's dressed in black and got his gym bag sagging with weight in hand and he's standing at my bedroom door.

"Get up dude. We gotta go," he says.

I says "Eddie, what time is it?"

He says it's one in the morning.

Mark guffawed. "So it's one a.m. and you guys are going to go cut the light with loppers?"

"That's right."

"Holy shit."

"Rock 'n' roll, dude," the stranger says. "Balls out and no fear. That was the deal. Live hard, die young and leave a good-looking corpse."

"If you say so," I interrupted.

"So here we go," he continued, explaining how he and Eddie parked in a secluded parking lot behind an apartment complex, got out and crested a small hill. "We crouch behind a row of bushes and look down below us about fifty yards out. Fire Station No. 5 is bathed under one-thousand watts of halide glory, white as the moon."

"Wouldja look at it?" Eddie exclaimed. "Just look at it."

"I'm looking, Eddie," I says. "I'm looking."

He opened his bag and took out a ski mask, fitted it over his head and adjusted the eye holes. Then he reached back in and pulled out rubber gloves and a huge pair of loppers.

"Holy shit!" Mark said.

To this I added: "Your friend Eddie was nuts!"

"Oh I know," the stranger said. "And you can be sure I asked Eddie if he was sure about this. Of course Eddie said *Hell yeah, Dude, Fuckin' A and buds as big as your fist*. And then he was off, creepy-crawling low and scrambling across the field to the light pole standing on the edge of the parking lot.

"He wasted no time when he got there. Kneeling at the base of the pole, he unscrewed the four screws holding the access plate, then removed it. And there was the electrical cord, that great spinal column of power that brought electricity to the bulb above him."

The stranger explained how Eddie looked up to the light and got temporarily blinded, then quickly looked back down again, shaking his head and rubbing his eyes.

"The power of that light was incredible for Eddie," he said. "I couldn't help but think of Icarus . . . or a moth, perhaps – a moth to the flame."

He said he then watched Eddie open the wooden lopper handles wide and push the steel jaws into the hole to cut the cord.

"From my vantage point behind the bushes in the distance I held my breath and crossed my fingers, saying *Go Eddie go!* to myself," he said.

The stranger paused there and shook his head. "Fuck!" he exclaimed.

"Jeez, Mister," Mark implored. "What happened?"

"When Eddie cut the cord there was a huge pop like a twelve gauge shotgun blast followed by instant darkness."

"Holy shit!" I exclaimed.

He paused a moment before going on. "Well, I waited and heard nothing. So I began hollering Eddie's name. Still hearing nothing, I ran down to the pole, and there was Eddie all passed out. I was shocked that firefighters weren't streaming out of the station because that light made one helluva noise going off.

"And man, I am like freaking out. So I grab Eddie under the pits and I'm trying to drag him off toward the bushes and I'm not even halfway there and *now* firefighters are streaming out of the station toward me. Oh, and there's some cop sirens, too. They're coming closer and closer."

"Jeez Louise and Holy Cow!" Mark shouted.

"God damn! That's a story! I cried, pouring him more beer. "So what happened?"

"Well, you know after all that they were waiting back at my place for me and had torn up the garden. My attorney later said he tried to get me in drug court but the cops had been busting so many growers that drug court was full."

"So then what?"

His mouth turned to a straight line then and I could almost hear the molars grinding when he shrugged and said, "I had to do three-to-five in the state pen."

"Wait a minute. How big was your garden?"

"Eddie and I had four vegetative plants about two feet tall each. So I ended up doing a year for each plant."

"May God have mercy on your soul!" I said. "That's so hard to believe."

"It was indeed," he said. "And days go by so slowly in jail."

"And those plants hadn't even flowered yet?" Mark asked.

"Nope."

"My sweet Jesus," he said. "I'm growing six plants legally in my basement right now because, you know, Colorado."

"But didn't you and Eddie get amnestied with all the other marijuana growers in jail when the Democrats took over?" I asked.

"I wish," he said. "Remember -- I went down when the Republicans were in charge. The four years were just for the plants. I copped another twenty for Eddie."

He no sooner said that when the temperature, which had been pleasant, turned cold again; so cold people began filing inside.

But Mark and I were transfixed.

"Eddie?" we asked together.

"I don't know how many amps Eddie ate that night," he said. "But I was dragging off a dead man. When the cops got me they charged me with accessory to murder, said I helped kill him."

"What the fuck!" I exclaimed.

"You fellers get it?" he asked. "I just got out of jail last night. I been locked up for twenty-four years in Nebraska."

And Mark and I are just freaking out, shaking our heads back and forth.

"Dude, I never heard of anything so unfair in all my life!" I cried.

And then some thunder-boomers bigger than the last ones came thudding down the street again: Boom! Boom! Boom! one after another like a string of bombs rolling over us, and before we could even stand a cold hard rain came tearing down.

I was almost in the door when I heard a huge ke-rack! and turned just in time to see the tree across the street split in two by a lightning bolt, then blown over by one of the strongest winds I've ever seen. I'm telling you it just wasn't natural. Not at all. Trashcans and everything rolling down the street. Windows breaking.

Sure everyone inside was talking about the mess of weather and taking pictures through the windows. I turned in all directions looking for the stranger, but didn't see him. Maybe he went to the restroom. I could

see the door from where I stood, so I kept my eye on it.
Guys came and went, but not the stranger.

"Hey Mark," I says. "Seen that old fellow we were
just talking to?"

"I was gonna ask you the same thing," he replied
with mild bewilderment.

"Did we ever get his name?"

"Don't think so. Don't believe he ever said."

So Mark and I sat there wondering if that guy we
met existed at all or if we just imagined him out of
some kind of stony-ass boredom. I stared at my shoes a
good bit before finally saying: "Well this ended up
being a strange night."

Mark said nothing.

I looked up at him. He was still puzzled.

"Mark, I'm not sure what just happened," I said.
"Are you?"

"No." he replied. "And that old guy . . . he just
disappeared."

"Damn, Dude," I said. "What's in this weed we
been smoking?"

Torched

Dude, strange story. You're not gonna believe it. So I went to our bro Ted's house yesterday. You know Ted, he took off for Oregon last year. He's back, with a guy who blows glass. That's right, a glass blower. Rasta dude. I kid you not; got dreads three feet long. White guy. Teaching Ted how to blow glass. Hell yeah, I'm serious. Is that crazy or what? Ted . . . he's always up to something.

So I called him yesterday morning 'cause I heard he was back in town, and he said, "C'mon over, we work every day in the shop."

And I said "What shop?" and he said "The garage in back of the house. Come check it out. I haven't seen you in The Day, brother."

So I go down to their little shack of a shop around mid-morning, and the guys are already in the garage getting started. First they were smoking a bowl.

Do I have good timing or what?

So I hugged Ted and met Dave, and we smoked some killer bud, dude. Wake-'n'-bake, you know what I mean? Then Dave said he needed to make some money and he turned and lit a nozzle on the countertop, about the size of a gun, four hoses feeding into the back of it -

- two red, two green: propane and oxygen. Blow ya sky-high if you aren't careful. Ted handed me some safety goggles. "Put these on bro, you're gonna need 'em to look at the flame. Watch Dave work now. He's pretty good. He learned in Eugene, dude. Yeah . . . Snodgrass . . . all them guys."

Dave went to a kiln in the corner and pulled out a 2-foot glass rod with a glass figure about the size of a pickle on the end of it -- just a raw, blob of a shape. But the embryo of a pipe waiting to be blown was inside the blob like a dream inside a brain.

He stepped on a foot pedal and a small blue flame shot out, becoming longer and broader until a big flame with a yellow core was blazing like a Jedi light saber. He said it was about 3,500 degrees. Is that hot enough for you? Dave stuck the glass inside the fire and bathed it, spinning the glass rod to keep the figure on the end of it whirling and twirling.

"Keep it still and it melts," he shouted. Rasta beats bumped from the box and the flame hissed; no, wait a minute; the sound was more like a roar, like when you put your ear to a conch shell on the beach and hear the ocean. Then Dave stepped on the pedal again, and the flame became a small, blue-burning heat tip, and he had this thin, glass rod in his right hand and he held the tip of it to the pipe's surface.

"This puts silver and gold on the clear Pyrex as base colors," he explained, and as he turned the glass in the flame, a faint, opalescent mother-of-pearl color emerged, like an Easter daybreak, man.

And this Dave guy kept saying "Heat it, spin it, blow it, show it."

Is that cool or what? So he held his left hand up with the blob of a glass piece in it. "This one's the girl," he said. Then he set his right hand on the torch. "And this one's the boy. Glass and fire; it takes both to make a pipe."

Sweet, huh? I'm telling you, this Dave guy is a trip. So here's the part you're not gonna believe. Two people show up, a guy and a girl, about 25 years old I'd say. Maybe married, I don't know. The chick? Pretty good looking, dude, pretty good looking, a real sister. Dude! She busted out an ounce of 'shrooms! No kidding. Well, what can I tell ya? It's been a while since I tripped, but those 'shrooms looked so sweet: not very big, but plump and with stems. Pretty.

So Ted goes inside to make tea from the mushrooms, and the guy, his name was Stephen, is an astrologer dude. Check it out – he starts telling Dave about his chart. I'm not kidding. He's going on like, "This is a good time for you to make money through creative enterprises."

Oh duh! I mean, Dave blows glass, ok? Even I can figure out that's where his cash will come from. And then this Stephen guy asks Dave if he's in a relationship now, and Dave says "Sure!" and Stephen goes: "Wow! Really?"

So we're all watching Dave shape the glass piece in the flame, taking it out, putting it back and keeping the temperature just perfect for shaping and blending in colors. And this flame is life itself, dude; it transforms the glass.

Ted comes back with a tray of mugs, and everyone but Dave and the astrologer drinks the mushroom tea.

There was a big ol' 'shroom in the bottom of each mug, and we swallowed them. Trippy, dude. And that chick, her name was Tara, she gagged big-time on hers -- chucked it right back up! It came shooting out of her mouth and hit the floor and I'll be damned if Dave's dog, a pit bull named AK, didn't leap off the sofa and snarf that 'shroom right down. No, I'm not kidding. And we're all yelling, "No, AK, no!" but Dave said "That's all right. AK used to trip 'shrooms all the time in Eugene."

Can you believe it? So now we're tripping with a pit bull. I look at all the glass on the countertop in front of the torch. Jars with different length glass rods in them look like multicolored spaghetti: ruby, pink, amber-purple and lots of thin clear glass. "Just straight Pyrex," Dave says.

And the light coming in through the glass door starts shining on all the different-sized and colored rods, making rainbows, dude, the colors all shifting. Awesome! Now get this. Ted starts showing me the kiln. He lifts the lid and explains how it works, but all I can do is stare at these four pipes baking in there. Maybe it's because I was tripping those 'shrooms, I don't know, but each one of the four pieces looked like a season.

Does that make any sense? I mean, one pipe looked like winter -- all blue, white and cold; reminded me of Finland. Another flared with summer colors -- yellow, orange, red; a pipe from Algiers or Morocco. The third was spring -- bright greens shooting through this long glass tube. Costa Rica, baby, tropical rain forest pipe on

a lily pad. And the fourth piece of course had your
autumn colors: brown, black and gold.

And I thought, "This guy's a friggin' genius, man."
And Dave keeps rapping about glass blowing, saying
how it's an ancient craft that goes back even before the
Egyptians. You want history? They got it. Dude, glass
blowing's been around as long as ganja and astrology.
Blowers even have their own patron saint, I kid you not.
Saint Anthony Abate. Straight up. Don't ask me how to
pronounce it smart-ass; I can't even spell it.

Then Ted really blows my mind. He whispers:
"Dude, I think Dave's girl just left him. Last night,
Dave was out at the bar with some friends and Tammi
came into the shop. We had a big talk. She told me
Dave doesn't 'see' her, but if she were a piece of glass
he wouldn't be able to keep his eyes off her. Then, a
minute ago when I was brewing the tea, I saw a yellow
envelope on the kitchen table. Addressed to Dave.
Sounds like she said adios with a Hallmark card, huh?"

Well, I'm listening to Ted tell me this stuff, and it's
blowing my mind because I saw a chick throw a
suitcase in a car and drive off as I was getting there. So
I whispered to Ted: "Redhead? Dreads like Dave's?"

"Yep," Ted says. "That's Tammi, all right. Long-
gone Tammi."

Can you believe it, dude? His woman left without
saying a word. Crazy. And he doesn't have a clue!

So, we go back to the workbench where Dave was
making a sweet bubbler for Stephen and Tara. I think
they brought the mushrooms into town, dude, 'cause
they were from the Northwest --Vancouver, Eugene,
somewhere like that. They said people trip 'shrooms

out there every day, dude. Can you imagine? Maybe they put 'em in the water. Wanna trip? Take a drink. Now that'd be livin'! The electric community! I'm there, dude, that's all I'm saying.

But anyway, this Stephen guy is telling Dave that since he's a Sagittarius and Ted is an Aries that it's natural they work with fire. Is that a trip? Fire signs working with fire. I don't know what sign that Tara chick was, but I'll tell you one thing: she was fire, dude.

So Stephen and Tara leave. Hell no they can't hang with us. Can't hang widda one-man gang, bro. Now we're tripping balls. Shit's meltin' everywhere; visuals coming on like gangbusters, and Ted, he's such a hoot, he looks at me and winks, then says to Dave, "So Bro, what have you and Tammi been up to?" And I look at Ted like, have you fucking lost your mind? 'Cause I know my mind was lost, dude, out wandering in the forest of foggy mushroom mist.

And Ted's crazy if he thinks I'm going to help him tell Dave that his girl's left him. Like what do I know about chicks? I know they're trouble, that's about it. And what they want from guys and what we want from them are two very different things, know what I'm saying, dude?

Then, check this out -- Dave starts rapping about women. "Yeah, man," he says, "Women. You just gotta treat 'em right. Like the glass here, dude. You gotta talk to it, work with it, make love to it."

And I'm thinking: "Buddy, what you don't know."

And Ted, he can't leave well-enough alone because here he comes again, a woodpecker hittin' the same

damn hole time after time: "Dave . . . there's something
I gotta tell you."

I wished there was something I could've thought to
say -- an interruption or something, but I stood there
drawing blanks.

"Sure man," Dave says, "what is it?"

"Well," Ted began . . .

"Dude!" Dave suddenly shouted. "Would you look
at this!"

The glass in the flame was a swirling cauldron of
colors: peach, berry, orange, cherry; spinning yet all
seemingly melting but yet, staying together, holding a
molten shape. Pure poetry, man. And then Dave starts
schooling Ted, 'cause after all, Ted's the apprentice,
right? And Dave's talking about this process called
fuming, where you bleed in the color rod to the clear
Pyrex shape you're working with. Of course, it's all
with heat, all with the torch. Dave said it all works
because glass traps fire's heat, cooling it and keeping it
for its own beauty. Is that cool or what?

So picture the planet Mars, all molten red. Now
shrink it down to golf ball size--that's what Dave had
suspended in the flame. The shape was becoming a
form. Then he did this etching stuff, where you take a
piece of iron about the size of a pencil, and you start
putting in swirls, curly-cues, swooshes– any design you
want.

For example, that astrologer dude was a Leo, so the
piece Dave had made for him had the lion symbol; you
know, the curly tail thing, all over the pipe. Talk about
technique; if you push too hard the reamer goes right

through the molten glass and you've ruined it. Touch and pressure are everything.

So this Dave is spinning and grinning, stylin' and profilin', and a guy shows up, Tim or something, and he says, "Hey, Dave, need any weed?

And Dave says, "Sure, need any 'shrooms?

And this Tim guy says, "Is the pope Catholic?" And they both whip their bags out and trade: an ounce of kind buds for an ounce of 'shrooms, plus Dave kicked him a piece. And I'm thinking, what a gig, you just sit there blowing glass all day and people bring you drugs.

Could you hang with that, bro?

So next thing you know we're huffing again. Talk about smoking from a phat piece, you should see Dave's personal bubbler. And this herb is killer: Willies, dude. I don't think those guys even smoke schwag; I mean, why would you if you were surrounded by kind buds all day long?

Now Tim is talking about the band Tammi is in, and how they're getting more gigs lately. He saw them play the other night.

"Dude," he said to Dave. "Tammi's good. She's got a great voice."

"Yeah," Dave said, "that's what I hear."

"What! You mean you haven't seen them?"

Dave's shoulders sagged a little and a sigh escaped his lips like he'd explained this one before and was getting a little tired of it: "No," he said, pausing. "It's hard to leave the flame, brother."

And the weird part was, at that exact moment we all realized that we, too, were staring at the torch,

riveted by its hissing and roaring and burning. I'm
tellin' ya, when he cranks that bitch it's a foot long. It
grabs you, dude. It grabs you by the booboo.

And check this out. AK, that mean old bastard,
he's lying on the sofa with his nuts hanging out
growling at everyone. So I'm all wrecked, and every
time I look at AK he shows me fangs. And I'm
thinking, Jesus, that dog's gonna rip my friggin' throat
out. I couldn't make friends with that dog for nothing,
but you know what I say: Never trust a pit bull tripping
'shrooms.

So here comes Ted again, talking about women.
The dude is a freak, what can I say. I can tell he's trying
to get it back to Tammi, and sure enough, he says, "You
and Tammi got any plans tonight, Dave?"

And Dave . . . it's obvious he hasn't even thought
about it. Like they say: you can lead a horse to water,
but you can't make him drink, right? I mean, Dave,
wake up and smell the kind buds, buddy. And while
you're at it, check on your woman, you know what I'm
saying, dude? TCB buddy -- take care of business.

So Ted can't get Dave to stop thinking about
blowing and start thinking about Tammi, which I guess
has been the problem all along. Finally Ted gets tired of
beating around the bush and he says, "Dave, there's
something I gotta tell ya. Can we go in the kitchen?"
and I'll be damned if the phone didn't ring.

So Dave's on the phone, and I look at Ted and say,
What are you . . . crazy?

And Ted says, "Man, his chick is with another guy and he doesn't even know she's left. Somethin' aint' right about that."

"Look," I says. "If you tell him, he'll hate your guts."

I'm right, aren't I? You don't want to be the one to tell your bro his woman's stepping out on him. It's like he'll blame you. Besides, I was tripping balls, dude, things were crazy enough, I can tell you that. Jeez, you shoulda been there.

Then Dave's off the phone. The guy he was talking to is coming over with three hundred dollars to have a piece blown. So the guy shows up and we all commence to smoking again, Dave matching his Willies with this guy's Kush. Yes, Hindu Kush, dude, you heard me. He had to have grown it himself. That's what I figure. His nugs were the size of strawberries -- covered with crytals! You can't buy nugs like that. No I am not lying. One hit, you're baked. Try it with 'shrooms, dude! I was torched. My brain was melting!

Speaking of melting, I saw the coolest thing. Dave's glass is coming alive under the torch. It's in the flame, and it's glowing like an aura or a rainbow, and the colors are shifting and changing, shimmering and twirling. What began as a shapeless blob is now plainly going to be a fat pipe with form, design and color. Around the rim of the molten bowl, glass melts and ripples like lava. And Dave's putting those color-dot-things around the equator of the bowl.

You know, those knobby things of color on glass pieces? He did a red one, then a green one, then blue and so on. And each time, he held the color-stick to the side of the bowl, working in the flame, varying its length, temperature and intensity. Then he pulls the color stick out with pliers, but the tip remains trapped in the sticky glass.

"Whoaa," he starts yelling. "Who's yo daddy? Who's yo Daddy!"

I'm telling you, that guy is a trip.

Now check this out. Dave picks a gold coin up with tongs, straight up twenty-four karat gold, and sticks it in the torch with the pipe. Molten gold flecks drip around the base of the bowl, which he keeps spinning of course. And on top it's all purple, crimson and ruby-colored. The bomb, dude, the bomb. Time kinda stands still when you're watching that stuff, know what I mean?

That's the part where he held the figure still momentarily and pushed the reamer into the glass. Dude, that becomes the bowl. Is that sweet or what? I have never seen anything like that in my life. And then you just poke your little carburetor hole on the side and presto! You got a pipe.

And all the while Dave's rapping about the trip to Jamaica he and some homies took a few weeks ago, talking about this swimming pool where the chicks went topless, and you jump in it from a ledge and swim over to a big wall of water vines and you climb up them and that's where the bar is. Would that be sweet or what?

So the guy with the Kush, he knew Tammi somehow, and he says to Dave: "Hey, who's Tammi's new boyfriend?" and Dave about came unglued.

"What the fuck are you talking about, crack ho?"

"Nothing . . . I just saw her having a drink with a guy at a bar last week. Chill, dude."

"At the Club Fusion, down on 13th?" Dave shot back.

"Yeah, I guess that was it."

"Her band had a gig there," Dave said. "The guy you saw her with was probably in the band, that's all."

But that did it for Dave. Agitation showed in his frown and furrowed brow, and at the same time he seemed confused. He glanced around the room like seeing it fresh for the first time . . . like waking up from a dream. He looked at us and the dog, and we're all holding our breaths like *Hey, What's up brother? Peace in the hood, right?*

And Dave scratches his head. "I'm gonna go show Tammi this piece," he says, and we're going "Yeah, good idea, bro, go show Tammi," trying not to laugh. I mean, it wasn't funny, but it was funny. Does that make any sense?

So he shuts the torch off and walks out, and Ted and I look at each other and go, "Oh Shit!" and start cracking up big-time -- not at Dave -- but because the incredible tension was suddenly gone.

And Ted says, "Can you believe it?" and I am shaking my head back-and-forth, rolling my eyes in disbelief, free of a great burden, the weight of the world off our shoulders, brother. The weight of the world.

So what's up Dude? Hey, I got some of those 'shrooms. Wanna party?

King Cannabis

He had endured the taunts of his friends long enough. Now he was trying to show them who really grew the best marijuana in town.

Mike couldn't take it anymore. He was fed up with his buddies ragging on his garden.

"Okay, here's the deal," he said, anger flaring in his voice. "You guys think what I grow is shit, tell ya what. Put your best effort on the table. I'll do the same. We'll call some friends and have a contest. See who grows the best dope.

Dan and Sam looked at each other and grinned: "Sure, dude, let's do it."

That's what brought them here, three months later, to the table in Mike's basement, gathered with fellow growers for what they hoped would be an annual tradition: the crowning of a ganja king. And why not? The five of them -- Mike, Dan, Sam, Josh and John -- provided at least half their city with kind buds. The way they saw it, they were entitled to crown themselves.

The rules were simple: each man would come to the table alone and straight (although half-drunk was allowed) and put down his best buds. They would be collected and put in jars, numbered but no names attached. Each person would smoke from his jar only, wait five minutes, then rate the marijuana. After that, the ganja king would be crowned and all the remaining buds and beer consumed.

Mike collected the baggies of fragrant herbs and went upstairs to the kitchen, where he put the marijuana in jars.

He knew he shouldn't get involved in such silly ego games with his friends. He heard them bragging downstairs, their voices rising above the music, about whose weed was going to lay down whom. Big men. Tough talk. Mike considered them friends, though at times they were certainly arrogant. Their mutual egos made the city growing scene a jittery mix of pride, paranoia and greed. No sharing, everyone on their own.

Like all good Type-A males, they had marked off territory and established themselves as chieftains, the ganja lords. Within each of their "districts" they'd set homies up in grow-houses -- places in nice neighborhoods, normal in every respect -- but inside, in the basements, ganja gardens 1,000-watt bulbs, fans, humidifiers and hydroponic systems.

Kind bud was $400 an ounce, more sought after than the Holy Grail, especially for those who could grow the green chronic.

Mike brought the bud jars downstairs and set them on the table. "Here you go guys, may the best man win."

He walked across the basement to the keg of Heineken resting in an ice-filled tub. As he refilled his mug, Sam and Dan ambled over.

"How's your mites?" Sam asked.

"Same as yours," Mike shot back. "Like I'm the only person who ever had mites."

"It's not that." Sam said. "It's just that you have so many."

"Yeah, weigh 'em by the pound," Dan chimed in. He stood beside Sam, grinning as usual.

"Don't your jaw muscles ever get tired from grinning?" Mike asked before he returned to the table.

Dan had that same dopey grin three months ago when he and Sam had unexpectedly stopped by. Mike was in his grow-room that night, as usual, watering, getting bitten by mites, cursing them, watching welts erupt in angry pink rashes along his forearms. Sweat made them worse. The temperature in the small room was 85 degrees – about as hot as it got. He had been burning 1,800 watts of combined red-and-white light from his high-pressure sodium and metal-halide bulbs all day.

"You mite bastards," he swore, setting down his jug of guano water to scratch. "I share my crop with you, and this is how you thank me. Greedy little plant suckers."

Mike had even switched to seeds lately so he could start with fresh, mite-free plants, but the marijuana still ended up covered with the tiny creatures. Having sativas didn't help. He was the only one in the group with them, mainly -- as far as he was concerned -- because his buddies wouldn't kick him down one of their fatty indica clones. No, they would rather laugh at him than help him out. Consequently, Mike's flowering cycle was tortuously long -- a quarter of a year -- plenty of time for mites to turn ganja dreams into webbed nightmares.

He squinted at some webbing under his magnifying glass. Mites raced madly along the gossamer trails, wild with abandon from feasting at the Cannabis Café on his plants. One fat brown mite, arms and legs spread like a skydiver impacting the earth, stuck face-down to a trichome, immobile, frozen in time on a sparkling drop of resin. Dry as a husk.

At least you went down with your boots on, little guy, Mike thought. *That'd be the way to go: face-down on a trichome as big as a boulder. Cause of death? Acute marijuana intoxication.*

He measured two teaspoons of organic insecticide into a gallon of water, shook it and poured the milky mix into his 3-gallon pump-sprayer. Time to show the mites who's boss.

Then the doorbell rang, and it was Dan and Sam. As far as Mike could tell, Dan didn't have many friends because he assumed other people didn't operate at his high level of intelligence. Neither was his reputation enhanced when, last year, he got a felony arrest for growing and tried to pin it on his girl, so the story went. Instead, she ditched him and split with their brindled boxer pup. Dan never held a real job -- not for long, at least -- and he didn't seem to do much of anything besides get stoned 24-7 on whatever was available: coke, meth, grass, hash, hallucinogens. Didn't matter to him.

Sam, on the other hand, graduated from the state university a year ago with a horticulture degree, although the only job he had was as a part-time delivery guy for a pizza joint.

Between the two of them they sported about 8 feet of hair -- the longest in town, getting stares everywhere they went; Sam for his black, wiry-haired mutton-chop sideburns bristling from his cheeks, and Dan for the creepy, vine-like tats on his arms and legs that appeared to intertwine with his veins. Dan was a bean-pole with devious, liquid-brown eyes.

The three of them smoked-out each other on their respective weeds, then Mike went upstairs for beers. When he returned, Dan was grinning. Mike saw that he and Sam had gone into his grow room and checked out his plants.

"What's up guys? You look thirsty," he said, offering them each a cold beer.

"Sam has something he's dying to tell you," Dan said.

But Sam hesitated, appeared reluctant, sipped his beer. "You know," he said after a while, "that you've got mites?"

"Of course," Mike said, meeting Sam's gaze. *What the frack*, he thought. *Give a guy a horticulture degree and he thinks he's a friggin' expert.*

"And you might as well cut everything down whether it's ready or not, because your plants have stopped growing. The mites have destroyed the meristems."

"Oh I know," Mike replied.

You arrogant bastard, he thought. *Like I'm going to cut my garden down just because you said to.*

Dan hovered behind Sam like a smirking vulture,

Why is he grinning like that? Mike wondered. That's when he snapped; threw down the gauntlet; issued the challenge to the smoke-out.

Mike had no sooner said it than he realized he couldn't win on taste. Although he dosed his plants with bat guano during their last eight weeks of flowering, they weren't much for bouquet. But he took a lot of comfort knowing that at least his buds didn't taste like fertilizer, unlike a lot of others he smoked. It was the stone, however, that he liked his own home-grown buds for. Quite simply, he knew they packed a punch. He could smoke about three bowls in his bong and be severely challenged no matter what he was trying to do. This was the weed Mike brought to the table today -- his entry in the King Cannabis contest.

Mike returned with a new glass of beer, trying to figure out which weed -- Josh's Kush, John's Willie or Sam's Mazeri -- he had given to whom. He did know that he had given his sativa buds to Dan, however. He sipped his beer and listened to Dan talking.

" . . . got this bro went to the Cannabis Cup five months ago in Amsterdam. Flew back with one seed between each toe. That's where my stash came from, the best in Holland." Dan laughed and slapped his knee, like he was the world's top storyteller.

He had been to Mike's house last year with Josh, whom they both knew as an old friend. Dan had pulled out some weed, kept saying check out this Northern Lights, and check out this Willie's cross, and they ended up smoking two fat hooters of the stuff, but nothing . . . hardly a buzz. Dan wanted to keep smoking, but Mike's lungs were cashed.

Mike remembered how, on the way out, Dan spied a bag of guano sitting on the shelf above the dryer.

"Oh my God," he exclaimed. "Don't use this stuff. It will burn your roots."

Mike had been using the guano for months now. It was 1-11-1, dry, and didn't smell. What wasn't to like about it?

Then Dan started going on about leaf color, and he paused to quiz Mike: "Okay, do you know anything about pH?" And the look he had on his face was like, "Hello, idiot, is anybody home?" No wonder the guy didn't have a girlfriend.

No, I know nothing about pH, Mike thought about saying. *I use the water that comes out of my faucets. Has a pH of 9 or 10. The plants love it.* Actually, two teaspoons of vinegar brought the acidity down to 6 or 6.5, ideal for his growing medium of compost, perlite, vermiculite, sphagnum peat moss, sand, ashes, blood meal, earthworm casings and lime.

Mike grew impatient. He stood and stretched. "Dudes, let's get rollin', and smokin', and tokin'!" he said, heading for the keg. When he returned, Josh had packed his glass piece and was lighting the nug. He took a huge hit and held the smoke in, then exhaled about a third of it slowly before stopping and inhaling; then waiting, exhaling another third of the hit, and so on, until the bowl was cashed. The corner of the basement filled with smoke.

"Damn . . . " someone muttered.

Josh looked stoned indeed. "Lucky you're not getting pulled over right now," John said. Everyone laughed.

Josh and John were, in fact, pulled over by a cop last month. They'd driven to a park on a Saturday morning and shared some mushroom tea with homies; then, driving home, Josh was nailed on a lane-change without signaling. He and John were smoking cigarettes by the time the police officer got to the van. They had the windows down and the vent-air blowing, but not all of that could conceal the dank smell of Josh's skunk buds.

"Dang . . . you boys be smoking the good stuff!" the cop exclaimed in mock-hillbilly drawl. He ordered them out of the car, handcuffed them to each other, and called for back-up with a drug dog.

Somehow the cops and the dog all passed the jar of brown psychedelic tea in the 1-quart Bell jar sitting on the dash. Josh and John still ended up with possession-under-an-ounce and paraphernalia charges, however.

The guys all respected Josh. He was the first of them all to grow, and his experience showed in his nugs. He grew the fattest, sweetest, stoniest buds any of them had ever tasted. Of course, it helped that his dad's friends -- the original growers from the '70s -- kicked down all their lamps and hydro kits to Josh when he was only 16. Everyone at the table owed Josh something connected to growing: either he let them borrow a light, or perhaps he gave them some fertilizer, clones, seedlings or advice.

Josh last saw Mike's garden about three months ago. A visit from Josh was an honor; he was not in the habit of getting out, mainly because he spent so much time in his own basement. Few people had seen Josh's garden.

"You're going to kill your plants if you use that salt," he'd said, noticing Mike's gallon box of Epsom salts.

"Yeah, I was thinking of using it, but decided against it," Mike lied. Actually, he knew salt was toxic to marijuana, but read about Epsom salts as a source of magnesium from a book on indoor cannabis growing. He'd used it a few times with no problems.

Josh also asked questions about flowering. "These buds should be fatter," he kept saying. "What are you using for fertilizer?" When Josh was satisfied Mike was fertilizing properly, he decided Mike's bulb's must be old. "That's it," he declared, "It's your bulbs. Gotta get new ones."

What the hell? Mike thought. The bulbs weren't more than a year old. And besides, did he go to their houses and criticize their gardens? No.

Dan looked at his weed--the sativa.

"Gee," Dan said, "I wonder whose herb this is?" But everyone chanted: Smoke! Smoke! Smoke! so Dan shut-up and huffed.

"Take it downtown, bro'," John said.

"Jesus," Dan spat. "Where's the taste?" He loaded yet another bowl. "Show you mo fo's how to smoke," he bragged.

"Taste?" Mike asked. "Your lungs are so covered in crud you couldn't taste a damn thing."

Dan exhaled his last toke and, with it, a raw, hacking cough.

"Jesus Christ, get an iron lung," Sam joked.

Now Mike was desperate to smoke. "All right," he said, "Think I'll step up to the plate." He couldn't take Dan anymore without being stoned. Besides, since they had made him the distributor of buds, he made sure he got Josh's buds. The first bowl Mike huffed yielded three hits. The ganja tasted both spicy and sweet.

"Wow," Mike said. "Not bad." He smoked another, then got dizzy. Someone else began smoking, but Mike was drifting away. He sat back. Pieces of old songs floated through his head. He felt elevated, as if he was sitting in a Ferris-wheel seat stopped at its highest point, rocking back and forth. He opened his eyes and saw everyone watching him.

"You okay, man?" Josh asked. He winked at Mike as a signal that he knew how good his buds were.

Mike ran his hand through his hair. "Jesus Criminy, I need a refill," he mumbled. He stood and tromped to the keg, arms out straight, Frankenstein-style. At the keg, he gulped a half-mug and refilled it, then leaned back against the wall watching the guys across the room. Sam was smoking his pile of buds. One, two, three. Good-bye Sam. Moments later he coughed his guts up and headed toward Mike and the keg.

"I'll pour, dude," Mike laughed. Sam was blasted; his eyes watered, his jaw hung.

"Thanks, bro," he whispered, watching his mug fill up and the white foam ooze down the side. Sam shook his head and let out a low whistle. "Hubba," he said.

Mike smiled. "I'll second that." He put a new CD in the boom box, then topped his mug off. He knew if he stood around too long that Sam would get to talking his ear off about growing, so Mike sauntered back to the table. John was the last to smoke. He was about to put flame to bowl when Dan, who had just stood up, passed out -- quick as a snap. Down like a limp noodle.

Josh leaped to his aid. " Dan . . . Dan," he kept saying.

Dan came to. "Whoaaa . . ." he said. " Head rush."

"You putting us on?" John growled, upset at Dan for interrupting his smoking. Dan stared back, said nothing.

Then John yelled: "All right, you mothers, not that any of you care, but I'm going to smoke now!" He grinned at Mike to let him know he was kidding, lit the fat bud in his pipe and huffed furiously. Holding it in, then spraying the smoke into the room.

Mike and the others laughed. "See you later," he said. "Bye-bye, John."

John closed his eyes and put his head in his hand like the sculpture "The Thinker." Everyone looked at him expectantly, waiting for his next move. He breathed rhythmically, soon opening his eyes and staring at his other nug on the table. A grin flickered on the corner of his mouth. He guzzled his remaining beer and slammed the stein on the table, then smoked his bud without coughing.

"You da man John!" Mike shouted. "You da man!"

John opened his mouth and a river of smoke poured out. One . . . two . . . three fattie smoke rings issued forth, the trio of donuts undulating in the air, dissolving slowly.

He looked at Dan and Josh. "What's going on?" They were sitting on the floor with their backs against the wall. "Dan, how the hell are you?" John repeated.

Dan stared at John, eyes big as saucers. "Oh, all right, dude," he mumbled. "Hey, got any munchies?"

Mike laughed back at John from across the table. "Catch one, dude?" he asked.

"Yeah, think I caught an eye buzz dude," he replied.

Mike and John were friends, but not like they used to be. Once they'd partnered-up for a long stretch of growing, but now Mike only saw him a few times a year. He knew John blamed him for mold that got into their crops. Mike could never understand why, though. He burned a 400-watt halide and a 400-watt sodium in his vegetation closet, ran a humidifier and kept plenty of air moving in and out. The humidity gage usually read 30 percent, and when the temperature spiked above 88 Fahrenheit, Mike shut off a light to cool the plants down. How mold grew in an environment like that Mike would never know.

Anyway, John spent more time with Josh now and there was nothing he could do about it. Josh's plants were clean of course -- no mites, no mold. Moreover, he had an extensive social circle, something else John no doubt found attractive. Like Sam, Josh hung out with the downtown crowd of head shop owners, band members and editors on the alternative newspaper.

Dan suddenly appeared like a jack-in-the-box. "Hey man, got any munchies?" he asked again.

Mike looked at him. Dan's mouth hung open and his eyes were vacant as an empty warehouse.

"Kitchen closet by the fridge . . . all the munchies in it . . . bring 'em down, would you?" Mike replied. He sauntered to the keg, noted his dizziness. *Slow it down buddy*, the voice in his head said. *Slow. It. Down.*

He was back at the table discussing fertilizers with Sam when Dan returned with an armload of chips, pretzels and crackers.

"Munchie time," Sam said, stuffing pretzels in his mouth. "Hey," he added: "Is everybody fucked up enough to vote?"

"Yeah," John said, "But first, a toast to getting fucked up." John was feeling no pain. He reached for the back of a chair to steady himself but missed.

Hear! Hear!" they shouted in unison. "A toast to getting fucked up!" Mugs were raised and ales quaffed in hearty draughts.

"To beer and women!" John toasted. He was quite a toaster when he got drunk.

"To beer and women," they shouted, some sloshing beer.

"Watch the floor -- watch the floor!" Mike admonished, to no avail.

"And kind buds!" Josh shouted. "Here's to kind buds!" "All right you drunk bastards," Mike interjected. "Let's vote. Everyone decides: best tasting, best stoniest weed."

They gathered around the table and began munching chips and pretzels. "The weed I smoked was very good," Josh said, and he proceeded to rate it on taste and stone. John followed in the same vein, and then Sam said: "I don't know about taste, but as far as stone goes, I've never seen Dan pass out before like he did a while ago. And now look at him."

Dan sat on the floor, his back against the wall, grinning happily. "What?" he said. "Why's everyone staring at me?"

"Hey dumbshit," Sam said. "Look what you're eating," and sure enough, Dan was working his way through a big red box of Original Milk-Bone Gravy Bones.

"I didn't know they were dog biscuits, man," he protested. "Someone musta mixed 'em in with the bags of chips." He paused, waiting for the laughter to die down. "Hey man," he said after a while, "You should try 'em . . . they're really pretty good."

"Yep," John said. "He's fucked-up, all right. Whose weed was that anyway . . . Josh's?"

"No," Mike replied. "Mine."

Everyone stared at him.

"Well I'll be damned," Josh said. "That was yours?"

"Yep." Mike said.

"Well," Josh said, "I think Sam has a point." The mutual assent was in the silence that prevailed. And then Josh rose and hoisted his mug to Mike:

"All hail the new king," he said, "King Cannabis."

To Smoke A Bowl

Braving a Nebraska blizzard to get a nug from a neighbor? Sure!

Cursing up a blue streak. That's what Joe was doing.

Why? Bedtime and he's outta weed.

Frack! That means a front-row seat on the insomnia roller-coaster roaring down the track at three in the morning, holding on for dear life while the paint peels off his face and he careens over the mountainside screaming with the rest of the lunatics on the ride.

Then 4:20 in the morning rolls around and Joe is doing what?

Going crazy? Eating the carpet? Chewing the sheets?

How about all of the above?

Now what?

Gotta text Buddy.

Say man. Can I get a cig for morning?

What's a "cig"? Two grams of weed inside a yellow American Spirit flip-top cigarette pack.

Luckily they're nearby: Buddy lives about sixty feet down the sidewalk from Joe in Buena Vista Apartments.

Joe won't get undressed and ready for bed yet. Buddy should have a cig on the porch soon.

Boy the weather looks bad out there.

Joe cleans his face, brushes his teeth.

Crap! No answer from Buddy yet.

Well, Joe tells himself. You best be off to bed, Old Friend. But man, would you listen to that wind howl.

Final phone check before lights out -- no response yet from Buddy.

Frack again.

Hey, no worries. Stay positive. Conceive it, believe it, see it. Right?

Now I lay me down to sleep; I pray the lord my soul to keep.

When I awake I hope I find some marijuana to ease my mind.

When Joe woke at three his first thought was that he'd miss the 420 Express this morning if he wasn't quick about his business. The mere thought of it set a shiver down his spine.

Quick! Check your phone Joe!

Cig on porch. Good luck getting It

Hooray! There is a god. Joe looked out the window. Oh my sweet Jesus. What the hell had happened while he slept? Piles of snow shifting and tossing and stacking themselves higher and higher outside. And the wind . . . what was with the wind howling like that with such shrieking and blowing? None of it looked any good.

Joe realized now this task would take some serious doing and when he opened the door he had to be ready to go. He thought how the cold would be so brutal he would just want to get on down the sidewalk, grab that American Spirit cigarette pack from Buddy's porch and scoot on back to the apartment. Don't think about it. Just go do it.

He opened the door to take a peek but the wind caught it so hard it blasted the door wide open and Joe could only shut it by getting his shoulder behind it and pushing it shut against the wind, which still came howling through the crack in the door.

These damn apartments! The Buena Vista units, more than a hundred years old, were originally built for Union Pacific railroad workers in the 1890s. Ancient, that's what they were. And cheap. Is this why renters here were the rudest, oddest rag-bag of humanity Joe had ever seen? He'd actually come to believe that all who lay their heads down each night at Buena Vista labored under some kind of mental malady, as if when they walked through the apartment gates a miniature version of Dante's Inferno opened up to a madhouse community of wingnuts and coo-coo birds escaped from mental hospitals and gathered here pretending to be normal.

Most stayed just a while and moved on but for more than a few folks the apartments were the last stop prior to the coffin-drop. Murdered. Suicide. Died of sickness. Tuberculosis, syphilis. Spanish flu of 1918. The list was a century in the making and long.

Joe knew nothing of this, naturally, although he, too, was on the skids. Shitty job. Shitty car. Shitty apartment. No girlfriend. But he did have Buddy down the sidewalk and a nug to get to even if it was so damn cold. So let's get going. *When the going gets tough the tough get going.* That's what Joe told himself. Same thing his father had told him; same thing the sign on the wall in high school gym said.

He pulled his cap down tightly over his head, cracked his door again and stepped outside. Oh my God it was cold! This time the wind, instead of blowing Joe's door open, sucked it shut with a SLAM! before he could grab it. Then an incredible blast of icy cold air pushed Joe along, and he slipped on the top step because of the ice he didn't see and went airborne.

Joe pitched head-first off the porch, used his right arm to break his fall and sprained his wrist when he hit the snow-packed concrete. He also came down hard on his right side, and that didn't feel too good either. He rolled over and lay on his back for a moment but the wind blew snow up his nose so he rolled over again and was this time staring at the ground on his hands and knees like a dog. What the hell! Talk about a bad start.

Where the hell is DeAndre, his next door neighbor, he wondered? Shouldn't he be walking down the sidewalk headed for the street to flip some crack? Dude was his own freaking postal service: rain, snow, sleet – didn't matter. DeAndre would be out on the curb making mad cash off chumps and bitches, slinging powder. But then Joe realized travel was impossible at the moment and DeAndre's customers would just have to jones at home alone in this blizzard.

Good thing Joe wasn't going too far or he would have worn his winter thermals under his jeans. He thought of turning around and going back, but on the other hand he'd just begun and if he went back he'd go crazy without anything to smoke for hours upon end.

Which is why he willed himself to go forward. Using his good left hand and left leg, Joe pushed himself back to his feet. Once again the wind shoved him along. He crouched low to present less of a profile but the raging torrent of air shifted and stinging needles of sleet pelted his cheeks as he stumbled down the sidewalk.

Not all apartment residents passed on to their final reward in the hereafter following the final coffin-drop. Some stayed as ghosts unable to cross over, trapped as ghostly wraiths in an ethereal purgatory. One was Sadie Mae Jones, 1875 to 1915. No sooner married in '93 to her Henry than he went and got killed down in the Union Pacific maintenance yard when a locomotive slipped its chock and rolled over him. Cut him in two it did. Then what was she to do? Well, she had seen the men's eyes follow her: some kind and loving, others lustful and lascivious. Knowing all this and more in her bones she began letting some of them into her bedroom, and herself, so they could get their little gush of pleasure and relief and she could pay her rent and eat.

Indeed, the men and boys would have stood in line outside her door if she'd a let them. They thanked her profusely and all concerned agreed she provided a community service for the lonesome, hard-working, handsome men and boys so far from home and down in the U. P. Yard. Poor Sadie with her throat cut and the ruffian what done it chased down the Missouri all the way to Saint Jo and disappeared into Kansas, the Jayhawk bastard.

Sadie Mae tapped on the window to get Joe's attention. The poor boy looked so cold, she thought.

And what could he possibly be doing outside in weather like this? She would have him in and fix him a cup of hot tea, she would. And throw a blanket over his shoulders.

Joe looked over at the window because he thought he heard a tapping. But did he see Sadie Mae? Not quite sure. Could he trust his senses at the minute? Oh hell no. So he kept going, as he had to because he was tough and toughs kept going. Besides: He was a man on a mission. He had a nug to fetch.

By God! The tip of his nose was so cold it burned hot! Joe hadn't checked the temperature before setting out. Why bother? It was cold and the forecast was for colder weather still. So there was nothing to check. This was February; he lived on the Plains; and the wind tonight roared and howled with a freezing numbness rivalling anything Siberia could throw up.

Hurry! Hurry! The voice in his head urged him. This was a tougher assignment than Joe had expected, and it was getting tougher by the minute.

He now wondered if he was getting snow blindness or hallucinations because Joe glanced over at the empty apartment window to his left where Dalton and Amanda lived until recently and he saw the previous resident, Mark Pendergast, who lived there and died from AIDS just a short year ago. Mark was one of many former NYC or LA drag queens come back home to Omaha to wait for the man with the scythe to cut them down and take them across the river. Mark had already told friends dearly departed: "See ya soon, fellas!" But not. He was trapped with all the other lost souls of Buena Vista and couldn't cross over.

Now Joe saw Mark's ghost standing in the living room looking out at him through the blinds.

Poor Dalton and Amanda. Moved in after Mark, then just as quick moved out and met their end on I-80 over in Iowa. Just kids, really. Dalton always dashing out his door, gun in hand, at the slightest sound out on Sixteenth Street; Dalton, who actually set steel traps out on the Missouri River to catch critters. And Angry Amanda, who walked with a limp because her last boyfriend ran over her with his truck and crushed her leg. Amanda with long red hair and stereotypical temper to match. Always shaking her cane at good-natured Dalton.

Joe was looking at the window so therefore didn't see the plant container blown onto the sidewalk that he tripped over. Once again he was stretching out his arms to break a forward-pitching fall; and once again he was skidding along in the snow, his chin an old iron-horse locomotive plowing through a snow-laden track before grinding to a halt on the sidewalk.

Frack!

He spit out the snow in his mouth and sat up. Jesus! What did a man have to do to get a nug in this world? Now his left knee hurt. At least the cold would keep it from swelling.

Suddenly Joe heard a pistol shot ring out. He turned to see Porno Paul behind his apartment window looking at him and grimacing in pain. Porno Paul had actually gotten himself a headline in the Omaha World-Herald a few years back: "Steakhouse Manager Shoots Self in Leg at Work."

Paul lost his job over that one. Heck, he almost lost his life, too. Single, bald, overweight and slovenly, Paul's hobbies were porn and guns, so it was natural that his dingy basement with a dirt floor was filled with disgusting magazines and assault rifles. He also strapped a pistol to each leg when he went to work in the restaurant, which is what got him fired because one day while cleaning one of the guns in his office he shot himself in the leg. Damn near killed himself. What the bullet didn't do the booze did while Paul was recuperating. He drank himself to death and his ghost never left Buena Vista.

Joe turned away from the sick bastard and trudged on, reaching the sidewalk where it split and went left and right around the circular fountain, the only thing worth looking at in the barren courtyard. In the middle of the fountain stood a life-size, white stone goddess -- a proud maiden with her head high in the air, a garland of flowers slung over one shoulder and a very bare and frozen right breast. Venus in all her glory coming out of the waves.

And just beyond Venus -- up on the left – sat Buddy's porch and, with any luck, the ganja nug in the yellow flip-top cigarette pack.

Joe was on his knees for a hot second before he could stand and steady himself against the screaming wall of air that kept trying to knock him back down. With a determined heave he stood, then pushed forward with his quads. The sound of a hundred tornadoes roared in his ears. His wrist and knee throbbed with pain, and his hands and feet were going numb so fast he was going to call them numb and number.

Be a Roman! He told himself. Remember the story about the Roman legion back in the day that came to the Rhine, built a bridge in ten days and marched across it to go after the Huns? *Be a Roman!* He told himself. *Build your bridge and get that nug.*

The wind, which had been in a kind of steady second gear now shifted into third, picking up speed and driving the wind chill well below zero. It was just terribly, awfully bone-chilling cold.

No matter. He was here now. He gingerly placed his feet one after the other up the four steps to Buddy's porch table with the dirt-filled pots from last summer where he lifted the back one up and there it was! The treasure of the Sierra Madre, the object of his quest: the yellow American Spirit flip-top cigarette pack with two grams of ganja in it. Check to be sure. Yup. There they were: little green nugs all snug and secure in a cellophane wrapper.

Now all he needed to do was get back to his apartment with them.

Joe's right turn off Buddy's porch to head home put him face-first into the violent air blasting at him with a high-pitched, furious scream. His face, already colder than he could ever remember, took an even icier plunge into a subarctic sea and his cheeks stung badly he couldn't keep his eyes open from the sleet pounding against them. Then his eyelashes and eyelids froze shut because he began crying from frustration.

For the love of God! What was with this weather!? The weather people on TV, those bastards, always smiling straight into your face and telling lies, goosing the weather moose for ratings. Joe never believed a word they said; only this time they had been spot-on. How dare they be right for a change! Of all the nights.

That's it. He decided then and there to call Buddy. His own apartment seemed so far away. And screw the time; screw how angry Buddy would be for waking him up at this hour. Joe had to get inside and get warm. He sat down, back against the fountain wall, and with frozen fingers tried to open his pocket for his phone.

His right hand had a glove but he couldn't use it due to his sprained wrist, and the fingers on his left hand were numb from cold since he'd lost that glove somewhere on the trek over. But that wasn't the worst of it. Joe felt sick to his stomach when he realized he'd forgotten to bring his phone.

A woman began laughing. Joe turned and saw Wanda Johnson, who many years ago lived in the apartment across from Buddy and made her money doing online porn videos until she met a guy once in the park for a blowjob and he strangled her. She was out on the fountain occupying the spot she used to sunbathe in. Wanda always drove the women crazy because she would come out near-naked and lie along the top of the fountain wall to catch some rays, her huge boobs barely contained and a shoestring bikini covering next to nothing.

Oh Josey Wosey, she says to Joe. *Come lay in the sun and play with me. I've got an itch the size of Tennessee.*

Joe did not and could not acknowledge her. Doing so would only be proof that he was losing his mind and seeing dead people. *Shake it off and get yourself together,* he told himself. He just had to keep going.

Straight and simple, that's all there was to it. *Keep going.*

The goddess in the fountain that on the way over had been Venus now revealed her true self to be a terrifying composite of all the trapped souls who had lived in the apartments over the last century: the sick-minded perverts, the mean and twisted sadists, the broken and hopeless suicides. Now all these people gathered force behind her eyes and channeled through them a Medusa gaze of two red laser beams, and Joe instinctively knew if they hit him he would turn into a frozen stone statue.

And here they came. He rolled over hard-right. The deadly beam just missed him, but swung around again. Roll, Joe, roll! Down the sidewalk he goes in his snow-induced hallucinatory dream, dropping and rolling until he's free of Medusa's deadly beams. Then stops.

Shit. Sadie Mae again, tapping on the window. *Come inside my little frozen bird.*

He paid her no attention, of course, because she didn't really exist, so he kept straining forward into the wind that pushed back against him. The cold cut him clean to his bones, and he wondered why life had to be so hard

Joe gained ground in spite of his bad knee. Suddenly, though, a blast of wind like he'd never experienced roared down the chute between the two long rows of apartments facing each other, and that blast caught Joe mid-stride and off balance, blowing him backwards into the row of bushes running along the sidewalk.

And then in some way Joe could not figure out, he felt a quick and sharp pain in his side and realized a branch in the bushes had functioned like a knife, poking a hole through his jacket and piercing his side. How badly he did not know. He knew it hurt and that he was doubled over and that he was colder than he had ever been before. And Sweet Jesus! how he just wanted to get home and smoke some of this freaking marijuana that was taking so much out of his frozen and snow-crusted hide tonight.

He was just horribly cold now. He couldn't feel his ears or feet. Joe remembered the poem "Invictus" by William Ernest Henry, a poem burned into his mind for all eternity thanks to his seventh grade teacher who made the entire class memorize, then recite it. *In the foul clutch of circumstance I have not winced nor cried aloud* and *I thank whatever gods may be for my unconquerable soul.*

Unconquerable soul. *Got that?* he asked himself. That must be your soul, Joe. When the going gets tough . . . . the tough get crawling.

Crawling? When did that happen? Was he really crawling? His knee was crashed; his side was gored. So yes . . . crawling.

Won't be long now. Home stretch, bottom of the ninth inning.

Then a naked girl jumped over him, a pretty thing about twenty years old with long brown hair blowing straight back in the wind.

Joe saw her once before, albeit with her clothes on, a few weeks ago. She was what Buddy and he called "one of Grant's whores." Grant moved in a year ago with the sweetest girl ever. Turns out she was too sweet for Grant. After she left he told everyone she broke his heart, which is why he turned into a party animal drowning his sorrows in alcohol and loose women; hence, drunk girls taking dares and running around the courtyard naked in the wee hours.

She was so tipsy when she ran over Joe she couldn't see him. He hollered after her as her naked fanny went bouncing off back to Grant's apartment, but barely a whisper escaped his lips and the wind blew away what little sound came out.

Joe thought that was so typical of Buena Vista Apartments, where hope came to die. There was *something* about living here. It was so pronounced that Buddy and his wife told Joe before he moved in: *Don't do it*.

But the rent was so dirt cheap. Hard not to move in, then, money being as tight as it was. That being said, once Joe moved in he knew what Buddy and his wife meant, for The Hand of Evil shoved itself up most everybody's ass the day they moved in, bringing out their worst instincts and turning otherwise decent people into cruel and petty human beings.

Joe found that out last year when he was recuperating from a horrible fall down the rickety basement stairs where he broke both bones in his lower right leg, the tibia and fibula, as well as the ulna in his left arm just behind his wrist. Months later, when he finally could go outside, Joe stood on his porch and did a stupid thing.

He thought he could go down the five steps to the sidewalk on his crutches; instead he went flying, having completely misjudged the geometry of his body weight and the arc of the pendulum of his crutches. High in the air he flew before coming down on his left arm, which broke again.

He was reminded of this incident because he was now abreast of Angelica and Armando's porch, the ones who watched him fall that day. When they saw him pitch forward and slam into the concrete they didn't run forward to help when he lay writhing in pain and crying: they turned around and went inside.

Armando was short and silent and she was large and wicked. When she gave birth, the girl was short-legged like her father and hairy like her mother; poor thing cried constantly knowing she was to be raised by them.

Armando was a roofer on a traveling crew that spent days on rooftops and nights in bars in Sioux Falls, Sioux City, Des Moines, Omaha, Kansas City, and Wichita, stuffing dollar bills in the G-strings of working girls on poles.

Angelica was a shop girl in a beauty salon. Her job was sweeping the floor clean of hair, fetching supplies for the beauticians, and keeping the restrooms clean. Lowest of the low at work, Angelica changed her demeanor the minute she walked through the Buena Vista Apartment gates. She morphed into an evil mix of Nurse Ratchet and Cruella de Vil.

Angelica's sister lived next door with her partner and was one-half of a queer couple who never spoke to anyone. They were sullen, angry and drank a twelve-pack of Coronas each night while ordering pizza and nursing an oddly misplaced persecution complex that all straight people hated them.

Joe imagined them with Angelica and Armando looking out the window at him, laughing at his misfortune and slapping their fat thighs with delight.

One night last year the lesbians and Angelica had come home from the bars around two a.m. and kept making a racket and drinking . . . right under Joe's bedroom window in the courtyard. And where were all the other residents? Why, cowering under their blankets. Those cowards would never confront a bully like Angelica. When Joe stepped onto his balcony fifteen minutes later and asked the drunk wenches to call it a night they went insane: middle fingers up in the air. Shouts of *Move Out You Fucker!* Real sweethearts, those ones.

Joe finally saw his apartment light down the sidewalk shining dimly through the blinding and blowing snow and told himself that he had to get on his toes and make this final run for the roses. He knew now how dire his situation was. Long ago his body had diverted the blood away from his fingers and toes to help maintain its core temperature, so Joe could no longer move his fingers, and his feet were frozen blocks of ice on the ends of his legs. Plus, Joe's cheeks and the skin tissue beneath it had frozen, and his nose was purple. Joe couldn't feel any of it. Neither did he see the ice crystals that had formed across his face. But he did realize his joints and muscles had stiffened up so much he was beyond clumsy. He was a frozen board.

Go Joe go! You simply must go.

Trying to crawl up his steps now . . . Who knew steps could be so hard? Hurts . . . so much . . . so cold . . .

Finally Joe thudded head first into the door, nearly knocking himself out. Fumbled for the key in his pocket. Difficult. Fingers frozen. The key. Where is the damn key? The key that . . . wait a minute. When the wind blew the door shut half an hour ago as he was leaving, it made him forget all about the key.

Joe had no key.

He also had no phone.

Joe just wanted relief at this point and he knew what that entailed but what could he do?

He got a little sad, then. God! His life had been so hard. And now this. He wanted to say he'd had a good run in spite of the setbacks he encountered and the enemies he accrued. But maybe not. That was a tough question. He would have to think about it. Just as soon as he took a nap. So tired now. That's what he'd do. He'd wake up from his nap, smoke some of the marijuana buds and debate whether his tiny little life in Nebraska had been worth a damn. Thirty-seven years old and cashing it in. Shit.

Now the ghosts of Buena Vista trapped with one another for all eternity gathered in a circle around Joe and locked arms. Even Medusa took a rare break from posing as a statue of Venus by stepping down and clanking over to Joe's porch. She sounded like an old thrashing machine and left a trail of broken white plaster chips. And at the moment Joe's spirit left his body, Sadie Mae and Mark, Porno Paul, Wanda, Dalton, Amanda and Medusa grabbed it before it could slip off to heaven. Thus, shrieking in delight with wicked laughter, they welcomed Joe -- their new playmate and the newest ghost of Buena Vista Apartments.

Life has gone on pretty much as usual at the apartments since that awful night Joe froze to death. On the surface world, people move in; they argue, they shout; then move back out.

And in the ghostly world, Wanda sunbathes on the fountain at Medusa's feet. Amanda shakes her angry cane at men while Sadie Mae turns around and comforts them. Mark stares out his window and Porno Paul shoots himself in the leg.

Then there's Joe. He crawls down the sidewalk in the snow when a blizzard blows up, clutching a nug and trying to get home to smoke a bowl.

See You Later

When Dame Fortune beckons, you drop what you're doing and follow.

I didn't know how the guys on the plane felt, but inside the airport our emotions zoomed from rock-bottom to sky-high. On my left, Amy, starting to cry; on my right, Becky, half-smiling as we watched a yellow tug push the loaded plane away from the terminal and the band members away from our lives. A few others in our group of well-wishers cheered softly.

Amy had put the brave face on when Paul kissed her good-bye and boarded the aircraft. She hardly shed a tear; that is, until he was out of sight. Now, as the plane lumbered to the end of the runway in the bright morning sun, her breath came in jagged sobs. Becky and I each put an arm around her, sandwiching her between us. We were too tired and hung over to say anything, but it did hurt to see Amy in such bad shape.

The band was flying to Atlanta. It's what we, their friends, all wanted for them -- in spite of knowing their departure would blast a big hole in our social lives. No, the contract was signed. Creatures of Habit was to play amphitheaters and auditoriums for six months in Georgia -- huge crowds compared to the turnouts they'd played to in Onawa, our hick city on the Missouri

River. This shot at the big time was what Creatures had been working for all these years, and the record deal in Atlanta was their first break. They had to go, and we all knew it.

Their farewell concert rocked the walls last night at the Frosty Mug, the boys belting out their usual alligator-caught-in-a-net music: wild, thrashing, intense; Joe beating all hell out of his drums, Ian pa-lunking the bass, Paul with the slashing rhythm and Mark with screaming lead and vocals: "I don't write the rules. I just laugh at fools," he sang. Bodies flew in the mosh pit, freeze-framed and mechanical-looking in the strobe lights, appearing to drown in tidal waves of angry music.

Steve and I smoked cigarettes and talked between songs. He was the bartender's dealer, so he was drinking for free. As a friend of his, I was too. "Hey," he says, "get a load of that." Amy walked in with three of her girlfriends, all 21 recently and having the time of their lives. Each wore blue jeans with a different-colored pastel tank top: peach, mint, lemon, cherry.

We waved and they strolled over, sitting at the bar like a row of sherbet ice-cream cones: two blondes, a red-head and Amy, who kept tossing her coal-black hair and flashing her startling green eyes.

We talked about the old days almost eight years ago when Mark, Paul, Joe and Ian got started. We were all beginning high school then, and those four were the ones in our gang who bought guitars and drums and actually learned to play them. Back then, when the band was practicing, we used to smoke bowls in the garage or the basement -- maybe even drink and have people over if someone's parents were gone. Hanging out with the guys when they were practicing or playing was always fun. And they got better. Pretty soon they'd written about 15 songs. By graduation, they were playing regularly. A few years later, Creatures of Habit was the metro's most popular thrash group.

Couples staggered back from the stage, away from Mark's raw voice through the amps.

Steve motioned to the bartender, then looked at me. "Whata ya think? These guys good tonight, or what?"

Yeah, I had to give it to them, they were sounding tight. Seeing Mark play was always fun because he went from being a buddy to being this rock 'n' roll guy, a heavy-metal guitar player, and it was like, *Wow, there's Mark up on stage*. Same for the rest of the guys. When you watched them play they became someone else.

After the bartender dropped off two more Jack and Cokes, Steve pulled a baggie from his pocket and set it on his thigh. "Hey," he said, "I got some kind buds." Sure enough, a nice bag. I could already smell those skunk buds.

"Jesus, buddy, be careful," I said.

I'd been watching the security guard at the other end of the bar. He began walking toward us, and a major jolt of adrenaline hit me. I stood up, ready to run.

"Bogie, 12 o'clock high," I said.

"Relax," Steve replied, "I smoke out with this guy all the time."

Go figure, that's what I say; still, I was a little nervous. Maybe it was the big white letters SECURITY on this guy's shirt. He came over and said to Steve: "You might wanna put that thing away." Steve introduced us, we talked, and somewhere we connected on guy stuff--hunting, drinking, military service: I forget. But I do remember that after a while he said he'd like to buy me a drink, and I said, "Buddy, you are a major stud," and he laughed and said "Fucking A," and then I was tossing down a fat shot of estate-bottled, blue agave, ass-kickin', tequila. *Bueno. Here's to you, amigo. Gracias, senor bouncer. Please excuse me now. The band is taking a break and I must go smoke out with them.*

In the band room behind the stage, Ian and Paul were already hitting a glass pipe while Steve loaded a bowl from his bag and got his pipe going around, too. Mark couldn't stand still. He'd gone from 100 miles an hour with his hair on fire to standing around with us smoking and talking.

"How do we sound tonight?" Mark shouted, hair dripping sweat and wet T-shirt sticking to his chest. Joe stood on the edge of the circle as always with Becky, his wife. Paul and I talked about the sound he was getting from his new white Fender Telecaster.

Amy and the bevy of beauties arrived, and she went for Paul. They had been going together about four months now. Of course she knew he was leaving in the morning without her, but there was nothing for her in Atlanta. She was only a year away from graduating from college; and besides, Paul hadn't asked her to join him.

I turned around and bumped into Belinda. She was a wild kid sister to us. *La chica loquita bonita.* Half-Sicilian, half-Mexican. Personality like a flame thrower. She flirted with all of us, and we were fiercely protective of her. We always kidded her, "When you want a real man, give one of us a call," but we all had too much fun hanging out with her to think of romance. Besides, Belinda could drink any one of us under the table, or at least meet us on the floor when we were passing out. Why ruin a beautiful relationship like that with sex?

Back at the bar, she joined Steve and me and started doing shots of Cuervo 1800, and sure enough, flames roared to life in her eyes, and I said: "Uh oh, slow down girl, don't get crazy," and she just held up her middle finger and grinned.

"Whatsa matter?" she said, "I thought you liked 'em a little crazy.." She hollered for another shot and tossed it down, then wandered off to mosh as the band began another set. Mark worked the crowd: "ARE YOU FEELING GOOD TONIGHT, ONAWA— Yeahhh!" and then off to the races, Joe laying down his mile-a-minute drum magic; Ian rattling the rafters with the low, bass notes; the red, blue and yellow stage lights distorting their faces; music loud enough to melt the paint off the walls.

People streamed through the door now that it was past 10. Mark and Paul jumped and slashed like maniacs, music ear-drum-popping, angry, intense; screaming into their microphones. Steve and I were back at the bar drinking Jack and Coke, lovin' life.

After three rounds, he motioned toward the door, and we walked out around the side of the building straight down the length of it to the back where a glen of trees offered refuge. We had just crouched in the bushes to burn a bowl when we saw Belinda running toward us. But she was running on the tops of the cars parked in a row alongside the building, leaping from hood to hood, denting each one in turn. Thunk! Thunk! Thunk! She caught up with us laughing and breathing hard. We dashed to the other side of the building, not wanting to be anywhere near the dented cars. I was furious at her, and for some reason she thought what she'd done was funny.

"Grab her arm," I commanded Steve, turning to see if we were being chased.

"Walk nonchalantly," I hissed at Belinda, getting on her other side. She needed supervision, I realized, too late. But I didn't want to baby sit; I wanted to party. Belinda was all lovey-dovey on both of us, trying to win herself back into our good graces. "C'mon," she said, tickling me, "Let's see a laugh." Steve and I weren't having any of her tricks, though.

Back inside, we dumped Belinda off with the bevy of beauties and I talked briefly with Amy about who was going to the airport in the morning to see the guys off. She seemed fine -- all smiley and happy. Amy had a nice, natural way of putting people at ease. I never could figure out why she got attached to Paul. With him, the band always came first. At least he was fair about it: he told her up-front. And she said okay, that was fine with her, she didn't want a serious relationship. Maybe she just wanted to date a guy in a band.

Amy's friend, Marie, came over. Marie was a shot girl at the Frosty Mug, treading the floor patiently all night in skin-tight black clothes, cover girl makeup, bottles of liquor swaying from leather holsters around her hips, selling shots for two bucks a pop. Your basic leather-and-alcohol sex-fantasy.

The band took another break and once again we crowded the room behind stage. The guys were dripping with sweat, but happy – very happy. Ian talked to his girl, a Vietnamese stripper, while Becky wiped Joe off with a towel.

"Yeah . . . here's to everyone who told us to put down our guitars and grow up," Paul shouted: "Fuck you!"

We roared and cheered, drinks hoisted high in the crowded room, the jostled beer running down our arms. Amy and her girlfriends converged on Paul and Mark. Mark shouted: "Here's to the last gig in Onawa!" and we all roared again. Marie was pouring free shots of Wild Turkey; then came time for Creatures' last set. We all got back out on the floor and the band was off to the races. So, of course, were we. Becky, Belinda, the bevy of beauties, Amy, Steve, me: drunk, stoned, spinning, jamming. Crazy fun. When the gig ended at midnight we helped the guys carry their guitars, amps and drums to the cars, and we all drove to Tom's.

Tom still lived at home. His father, rumor had it, was an accountant for the Midwest mob who still traveled frequently to Chicago and Kansas City. We walked quietly around to the back of the house and entered the den through the sliding glass doors. Some of us went to the bar at one end of the large room and began drinking, while others began playing pool. I sat at the bar with the guys, all of us watching every time one of the girls bent over to take a long shot at the table, making remarks about their breasts, making them self-conscious, acting like jerks, trying to make them blush.

Tom kept checking on people at first. He fussed at someone puking in the bathroom, then settled a fight between a couple in the process of breaking up. A few minutes later he shooed another couple out of an upstairs bedroom. "You're gonna haff ta shcrew eacsh uh-zjer somewhere elsh," he slurred.

Mark, Paul, Becky and I sat down to do tequila shots, and Tom and Mary joined us. Soon, Tom grabbed one of Mary's lipsticks and wrote SLAYER on her forehead and, for some reason, she let him. Then she rose triumphantly and grabbed the lipstick from Tom, who realized too late that he was in trouble now. She did him up like a red valentine, which got us all to laughing pretty good.

We drank more tequila and orange juice, and Mary announced for around the fourth time that night that she had to pee. For some reason, every time she went, he had to come with her.

"C'mon Tom," she said, and they staggered off to the bathroom together, Tom with sunken shoulders and the look of a resigned man.

When they returned, the argument that had flared up between them was a red rage on their faces. They were literally grinding their teeth at each other. This was par for the course. For them, there was no middle ground. They were either fighting or making up, and it was a sure bet that the drunker they got, the worse they argued. Problem was, they got drunk just about every night. Tom escaped to the bar and began slamming drinks with the guys while Mary sat with us in a huff, throwing angry darts at him with her eyes.

A couple named Sean and Marcy showed up. They were on a three-day coke run, financing the powder with cash from a half-pound of weed she'd brought up from Texas. "Hey everybody," Sean said. "Remember Marcy? She used to live here."

Marcy walked over to the pool table. "Hi y'all. Anyone wanna buy some loco weed?"

I'll tell you, that chick has balls. She took a bunch of bags out of her purse and laid them on the pool table: nickels, dimes, an ounce. Gone in minutes, replaced by a pile of green bills. Then she and Sean were in the bathroom making the razor blade and mirror go click-click-click, a sound followed by sniff-sniff-sniff. That Marcy, we hadn't seen her in over a year and it was just like old times all over again.

Then Belinda arrived, cheeks flushed, breath heaving. "Hey everybody, guess what I did on the way over here after the show?" she shouted.

"Wrecked your car?" I ventured.

"No," she shot back.

"Got a ticket?" someone else ventured.

"Fuck you," she shot back again.

She came toward us in the light, and we all simultaneously noticed her busted lip and bloody gums.

"Broke up with your boyfriend?" Mark asked.

"Yeah, but something else, too -- "

"Is that how you got your busted lip?" Paul interrupted.

"Yeah, but listen," she implored . . .

"Goddamn it fellas, saddle up," I said. "We got some ass to kick." We guys began getting up and grumbling, but Belinda shushed us back down.

"No, check it out," she said. "I already took care of it. When I broke up with that jerk, he called me a bitch and slapped me." She faltered, began crying. "I was trying to be as nice as I could to him and that mother fucker punched me! Can I have a drink?"

Paul brought her a cold beer.

"So I kicked him in the nuts as hard as I could," she continued. "Got him good. He doubled over on the ground and cursed me. I left. I went to my garage and got the gas can in -- "

"Oh my God," someone said. "Don't tell me you --
"

"Fuckin' A!" she exalted. "I drove to his apartment complex, waited until his bedroom light went off, then splashed his car from bumper-to-bumper."

We stared at her incredulously. "No way," someone said.

Becky brought Belinda a cold washcloth for her lip.

"I swear to God," she replied, gulping the beer, "no one fucks with me like that."

So what happened? we all asked.

"What happened?" she cried, laughing so hard she fell over the couch, rolled off the cushions and onto the floor. "What happened?" she repeated again. "His car exploded -- that's what happened!"

We roared with laughter -- even talked about driving to the guy's apartment to check out his smoldering wreck, but Amy slid the glass door open and tip-toed in, fresh as the dawn and lovely as a doe, even at 3 a.m. We all give her props when she takes out three nugs the size of olives, all sugar-dusted -- green, red and brown, sits on Paul's lap and beams like a kid who just brought an A paper home from school.

She holds the pipe to Paul's lips to give him the first hit. "C'mon baby, you know you want it," she moans, leaning into his face with the pipe next to her breast. *I want it if he doesn't*, I felt like saying.

Amy's kind buds on top of Marcy's Texas weed hit us all pretty hard. We turned the lights off, lit candles and watched shadows dance as Pink Floyd's Dark Side of the Moon played. A bag of 'shrooms sat on the table, but I was too drunk and stoned to bother tripping. I laid back on the sofa, eyes half-closed, and suddenly there was Marie, across the room on a sofa. But she wasn't a shot-girl anymore. Her hair was down and her makeup was off and she had changed into jeans and a loose-fitting top. She looked sweet and normal instead of like a whore. I watched a high school senior try his game out with her and laughed to myself. Men were a deck of cards to Marie. She shuffled and dealt them like a Vegas dealer working hicks from the sticks.

Meanwhile, Jack Daniels and Jose Cuervo were trying to knock each other out in my stomach, and I switched to water, hoping to quiet those bad boys down.

Paul followed my lead, and somehow we got to talking about the night last summer when we were all

down at the marina on Ian's dad's yacht. That night, Ian
and Donald, another one of our homies, came back
from the marina bar with bloody noses and swollen
eyes. We'd been drinking gin all afternoon, so we got
pissed in a hurry. We practically ran to the bar, saw the
three assailants sitting at a table and flew at them like
wild men--punching, ducking, kicking and swinging.

I broke one guy's nose, but I also took a punch to
the jaw that rocked my world. The owner jumped over
the bar with a baseball bat and stopped us from tearing
his place up and running his customers off. Then he
banned us for the rest of the year. We didn't care.

Our testosterone level was sky-high. Mother
Nature matched us. The temperature fell 20 degrees and
thunderheads boiled up with booms and cracks. We
were soaking wet by the time we got back to the yacht.
Booze to dull the pain. That's what we needed. And ice
for swollen jaws, cut knuckles and stiff drinks.

The rain slackened, and by 1 a.m. I was ready to
call it a day. I told Paul I was gonna start his car 'n' get
the heater running 'cause it was cold outside. "Gimmee
your keys," I said. "You're my ride home." I staggered
off the boat and down the pier. The Missouri was swift
and powerful, angry and roaring in its banks. Our cars
were only about 6 feet from the river's edge. Hastily, I
put the clutch in to start the motor, but Paul's old car
rolled forward and slid down the river bank so quickly
that I was in the water before I could react.

I remembered then that Paul had mumbled
something earlier in the day about a busted emergency
brake. But that was all academic now because I could
not get the door open! Water rushed in through the

ancient floorboards, surging past my waist, racing for my chest. The engine was an anvil! The car plunged. I put my feet against the passenger-side door and, using all my leg force, pushed against my door. Nothing! Then I had to hold my breath because the river filled the car.

How fast can a man die? It hit me that I was about to find out. Scant moments ago I'd been sitting on a yacht getting pleasantly pickled with booze and ganja; now I was drowning. Life images flashed before my eyes, just like I'd always heard they did when you die. I saw my mother, father and sister, and I was crying and apologizing to them for dying like this when suddenly from somewhere far away I heard pounding, someone pounding on the window from outside, and a hand tearing at the door, pulling.

I pushed once more, weakly. Almost out of air. My last chance! The door cracked open. The hand grabbed my arm and pulled, and I pushed my way out to freedom, clawing for air, gasping for breath. Paul had just risked his life to save mine.

Amy, whom Paul met shortly after my near-drowning, had never heard the story before. "Wow, that's crazy," she said, gazing at Paul like a lovesick puppy. Then she threw her arms around him and gave him a kiss on the cheek. "My hero!" she exclaimed.

Somehow, 3 a.m. had rolled around. Half the crowd was gone, leaving about a dozen people. We had already figured we'd be up most of the night. Departure time for the plane was 7 a.m., so we needed to leave for the airport in three hours. Paul and Amy slipped away to an upstairs bedroom, as did Mark and a striking blonde none of us had met before, one of Amy's friends.

Then there was me and the guys: Jeff, Pete, Mike, and John. The Diehards, the Brew Crew, the Womanless Ones. We sank into the sofas and began watching a Jimi Hendrix video, Mike twisting a joint of schwag and me dozing off watching John and Pete eat more mushrooms.

A few hours later when it was time to go we were the walking dead. Heads pounding, stomachs heaving, throats dry, we drove to the airport in a five-car caravan. The aircraft was entirely boarded by the time we ran down to the terminal. Rush, rush, no time for good-byes. Just get on the plane.

It was almost over. In a few days we would be rested and healthy again, and Creatures of Habit would be a memory.

The airplane reached the end of the runway, turned without waiting and accelerated. Amy caught her breath.

Don't do it, I prayed. *Don't cry harder. Save your tears for someone who loves you.*

And what comes out is more of a sigh than a sob, an attempt at composure. The plane arcs up and zooms off, and I watch Amy pull herself together.

"Good-bye, Paul," she whispers. "Hasta la vista."

And something in the way she says it gives me a sense that she is going to be okay.

At last. Maybe now those flashing green eyes will see me and I can have a chance with her.

Slingin'

You gotta gun and I gotta gun so bring it on, tough guy, 'cause I ain't backing down.

Tony was getting out of his car at the quick shop to buy more beer when a car with three black dudes in it screeched to a halt beside him. Two of the guys jumped out, grabbed Tony and shoved him back in his seat.

One got behind Tony and punched a pistol barrel into the base of his skull. The other guy shut Tony's door and leaned so far in through the open window that the soggy toothpick jutting from his lips poked Tony's nose.

"Don't move, bee-atch," he drawled. Tony recoiled at the slaughterhouse-rotten breath.

He wondered if someone was playing a joke on him. If so, it wasn't funny.

The black at the window lowered his arm and Tony heard a click and felt a switchblade thwack open against his stomach.

"What's going on?" he asked. "Who the hell are you guys?"

"Shut up!" the black guy barked, sliding his blade along Tony's belly until he saw the white boy wincing and twisting with pain. Then he knew his knife was biting the cracker properly, teaching him respect.

"Nigga man in charge now," he growled. "Comprende?"

Tony grunted acknowledgment and flexed his abs as hard as he could when he felt the knife sting open about a half-foot gash of his skin. And all the time, the guy behind him kept jerking his head and ramming it back into the gun barrel. *Please . . .* Tony thought, *tell me I'm dreaming.* But his stomach stung like hell and his T-shirt was soaking up blood and he knew this was no prank. This was the real deal.

"Mutha-fucka," the guy behind him said, "Yo brains is gonna be on the windshield if yo so much as blinks yo eyes."

"All right, all right," Tony said. "You got me. Take it easy, wouldya?" The man with the knife folded it, strolled around the front of the car all casual style and got in beside him. Tony was stunned. These bastards had taken him down in about 10 seconds.

"Lookie here, bitch," he said, "We hate us some white boys. And it will be our pleasure to kill you. But not now. First, get us outta town. Go west. Or I'll stick this knife so far in your ribs it'll come out the other side."

"What did I do to you guys?" Tony asked. Would you talk to me?"

"Oh, you ain't done shit to us, white boy," he said. "We just payin' back a favor, that's all. And don't be raisin' your voice, bitch."

The tone in his voice said it all. Rotten Breath was heartless, a regular-old drug-dealin', pimpin', robbing, murdering son-of-a-ghetto-bitch-crack-ho.

The kid in back screwed the pistol barrel into Tony's neck again: "Start driving," he commanded. "Now."

"I will if you get that goddamn gun away from my head!" Tony said.

That son-of-a-bitch, he thought. *If I get out of this I'm gonna make him pay.*

Tony glanced in the rear-view mirror. The kid looked even younger than Rotten Breath. He kept sniffing and wiping his hand across his runny nose, his fervent eyes burning with whatever mix of drugs he was on. He was Powder Eyes, eyes of no mercy.

Tony pulled onto the highway, feeling the color draining from his face faster than water from a busted radiator hose. His assailants' smells of liquor, BO and blunts were making him sick to his stomach. *No wonder,* he thought. *It's frickin' sliced open.* He put his hand over the wound and held his shirt to it. His head spun around in dizzy-sweat.

Get a hold of yourself, he thought. *Conquer panic. Think clearly. You are in trouble, big trouble. Take deep breaths.*

Okay. They were going to kill him. For what? In his side mirror he saw the third black guy following them. Where's a friggin' cop when you need one? His kidnappers had chosen a good time. Soon it would be dark.

He drove west somberly, wondering how he got into situations like this. Perhaps he should have changed his ways long ago while he was ahead of the game. He knew the Lords of Karma had been tapping on his window for some time, trying to get his attention.

But he was always too busy working or having fun to stop, slow down, and listen.

Tony had thought about quitting dealing after he was robbed and shot last year. After all, there's nothing like a slug to slow a guy down. He had gone to sling some weed in the North O Ghetto, and the gang-bangers stopped shooting each other long enough to pop a cap into Tony, grateful for the opportunity to blow a white boy away for a change.

But Tony wasn't down for long. On top of a miraculous survival he added an astonishing recovery. Because the bullet was too close to his heart, no doctor would risk surgery. In time his body adjusted to the leaden invader. The muscles grew around it, the bruise faded and Tony actually forgot he carried a bullet in his chest.

Later, he got a tattoo of a target with the rings circling the hole where the slug had tried burrowing into his heart like a determined mole. His homeboys all thought the tat was the bomb, and he enjoyed the notoriety so much, and the reputation it brought, that he bought a pit bull, a Ruger 9 mm and slews of rapper CDs.

Goin' to the Hood to kick some ass," he'd brag on Saturday nights when the usual gang of around 10 people was at his place partying; Snoop, Tupac, Cypress Hill and other hoodlum music booming off the walls; people drinking gin and juice; the women wearing their skimpy cocktail dresses, guys hanging with the droopy, baggy jeans; everyone acting bad and black, sexy and tough.

Invariably someone would ask Tony to tell the story about how he had gone to the ghetto to sling an ounce to an old high school friend and got shot in the chest by the friend's brother -- shot for an ounce of kind buds, then driving to a pay phone and somehow dialing 911 and gasping his location before passing out.

Tony thought tonight was worse than back then. Last time he got capped he had no time whatsoever to think about it. He was sitting in his car and BLAM! He was shot from behind. Tonight, however, he had time to think, time to ponder his imminent demise. Tony turned on the headlights. How would they kill him? Heck, would he even be found? After all, they were headed for terrain of rolling fields laced with numerous streams and gullies, perfect ground for disposing of unwanted stiffs.

What if they killed you and just left you lying there? Put you on your knees along a creek bed and blew a hole in the back of your head. *Face down in the dirt, buddy: face down. Finito.*

He drove past the mansions of the city's wealthy elite, all lighted and warm behind multiple security barriers: a wall around the neighborhood; code-controlled entry gate; neighborhood watch program; home alarm systems. Then, the plains with corn and wheat on either side of the road standing dead still in the fields on this sweltering July night.

Nothing stirring. The road narrowed to two-lane traffic. Powder Nose sniffled again and grabbed Tony's collar. "Do the speed limit," smart-ass. "We got other things to do tonight than kill you."

Pardon me all to hell if I'm not in any hurry to get shot, Tony thought, nudging the speedometer to 50 mph. Goddamn his lousy luck! It kept slamming into him from behind like a multicar pile-up in fog, one crash after another. From getting shot last year to this bullshit now; and a few months ago, an incident nearby his old high school:

His homeboy, James, made a deal to sell an ounce of weed, was a little nervous about it and asked Tony to back him up. When they went to make the deal they pulled into far opposite spots of a parking lot in a small residential park where guys used to fight after school. Tony opened his glove box and placed his Ruger on the passenger seat of his Mazda, slouching low behind his tinted windows when he saw a car pull up to James'. Two white-boy wannabe gangsters got into James' car. Almost immediately, Tony saw two red lasers flying around. Glocks and gun sights! Tony cocked his 9 mm, dialed James' digital.

"What's up? You getting jacked?"

"Uh, yeah, I think so," James replied. Then the phone went dead. Later he would say he sounded foggy at the exact moment when Tony called because one of the punks had just smashed his Glock into James' head while the other one grabbed the ounce of weed between his legs and bolted from the car. High school kids with guns.

Oh geez, Tony had thought. Don't kill James. Not over a bag of dope. Please. James was the youngest of the group. Tony almost jumped out of his car with his Ruger blazing to prevent the two punks' getaway, but he thought about all the houses surrounding the park and realized he would be an idiot to start blasting caps.

So he watched them drive away with an ounce of organic-fed, Dutch-Willies-cross. Mouth-drooling buds that cost him $300 wholesale, aroma that'd knock your socks off, stone that'd make you flat goofy. Buds you'd stand in a long line to score; would walk a mile for. Gone! And those little hoodlums got them for free-- ripped him off an ounce of kind buds.

Teach those bastards a lesson. He was 6'2", 220 pounds, not exactly a shrimp. He had to scare the hell out of them for robbing him. The magnitude of their disrespect was astounding. A lot of dopers at the high school knew Tony was the man when it came to scoring because they were sophomores when he was a senior. He relished his role and its benefits. He always had girls over to party, and whenever some of the kids scored really good dope they usually came over to Tony's to impress him with it.

Then there was the embarrassment factor. Earlier that night when the gang was partying at his place, Tony was basically acting bad, cleaning his gun, clicking the hammer and showing people how the pistol worked. James kept shooting glances at the clock and playing Tupac loud, and pretty soon everyone felt nervous and tense. They all knew Tony and James were going out to sell some of the dope they'd been smoking lately. Tony scored two pounds of it just a few days ago. Coming back later that night and telling their homeboys and girlfriends that they'd gotten ripped off by high school kids had been humiliating, and Tony and James stayed up late, draining a fifth of tequila and plotting revenge with the Ruger on the table and murder in the music.

But now, driving west on a barren Nebraska highway, Tony realized that he might not live long enough to extract his revenge; that, unbelievably, his time on the planet might be up. He looked in his rear-view again. The old red car with the third black guy in it followed at a distance. In the sky, a crescent moon shed hardly any light.

"Turn off the road up here," the kidnapper in back said. He relaxed his grip on Tony's collar and waved his pistol toward a dirt road to the right.

I could grab that pistol, Tony thought, but then what? Three guys and a loose gun? That wouldn't work. But he had to make something happen. His Ruger was in the glove box. Could he get to it? He knew if he kept letting these guys take him down these small roads that his situation would be hopeless. Not that it already wasn't. *Face down in the dirt, buddy. Or floating down the Platte.*

"Hey," he said. "Whataya say we go to my place and chill out with some lines?"

"Ain't gonna be none-a dat," Rotten Breath said.

"All right, how 'bout we burn a joint right now?" Tony countered.

"How 'bout you shut up, bitch," Powder Nose said.

"Yeah, take it easy, white boy," Rotten Breath added. "Ain't nothin' you can do about it no mo. When it's your turn, it's your turn. Dat's all dare is to it."

"Man, tell me something, would you? Give me a clue," Tony pleaded. "If you're gonna kill me, don't I have a right to know why?"

"Cause dead men don't tell no tales," Rotten Breath said.

"Yeah, an' dey don't testify in court neither," Powder Nose giggled.

"Hey, shut up, bro," Rotten Breath told him.

"Court . . . what does court have to do with this?" Tony asked. And then it hit him. Recently a witness to his shooting last year had come forward, providing enough evidence for a preliminary hearing. Tony was supposed to testify next month as to what he knew about his attempted murder, and he certainly knew who did it because he had partied with them before.

"It's Dante Woodgate, isn't it?" he said.

Dante was the bastard who set Tony up when he was shot.

"Bingo," Rotten Breath replied. "Now just keep driving." He looked around absent-mindedly, then opened Tony's glove box and saw the Ruger. "My, my," he said, pulling it out. "Is you a bad-ass white boy?"

Tony shook his head no.

"Maybe you is a depressed white boy. And you drove your dumb ass out to the boonies to end your miserable life."

Tony remained silent.

"Dat's da ticket. Shoot you with your own gun and it looks like a suicide." He waved the pistol around, then placed it to Tony's temple.

"Sound good to you?" he asked, chuckling and sucking his toothpick."

Tony cursed silently. Now they had two guns. They had taken him by such surprise that he didn't have time to get his piece out of the glove box. Not good. He had to think of a way to outsmart his killers. The clock on the dashboard read 10 o'clock. He reckoned he had about half an hour to live, that by midnight the black bastards would be puffing blunts and smoking rocks with crack-ho's, bragging about how they did a white boy in, made the little bitch beg before they blew his brains out.

"Say, cuz," Rotten Breath said. "Give papa his bottle." Powder Nose pulled a half-pint from his pocket and handed it to him. Rotten Breath guzzled the whole thing. "Yessir – vitamins!" he exclaimed with a whiskey belch, rolling down the window and flinging the bottle into a corn field. "Whoo-eeee!" he yelled. "White boy gonna die tonight!"

Terrific, Tony thought. *Rotten Breath, a booze-hound, is getting up his courage to kill me.* Tony realized there was no guarantee that his end would be quick and painless. Maybe Rotten Breath and Powder Nose were sick fucks and meant to humiliate him before finishing him off. He slowed down and turned onto the dirt road. The guy in the car behind them followed cautiously. They had him boxed in good, he had to admit. This was all new for Tony. Usually he was the guy who called the shots, set things up. The order-giver and favor-granter. Tables reversed tonight buddy. Whatcha gonna do, gonna do?

Sure, he fashioned his life after a rap-song image, and in the main, made out like a bandit. Yeah, the phone rang too much sometimes. That was annoying. Of course, he could -- and often did -- shut it off. And he never kidded himself: dealing weed beat the hell out of working at a real job for minimum wage. He also enjoyed the prestige that came with slinging. People called him, not the other way around.

But tonight . . . Whatcha gonna do? Take the bitch-bullet, or fight like a man?

Tony had slowed down to about 20 mph on the dirt road. He knew enough local geography to realize the guys probably intended to go to the river whose tree-lined banks had provided cover over the years for people to picnic, satisfy their lust, skinny-dip, hold high-school keggers, commit suicide, or murder someone.

Now or never, brother. Use it or lose it; move or die.

Suddenly the things he had to do if he wanted to live popped in his head like a flash, and he saw the whole plan instantly, crystal clear: getting out of the car, running through fields, bullets whizzing around him. Ducking, hiding. And, if his luck held out, escaping and living.

Now Tony. Do it now.

He jammed the gas pedal and the car leapt forward, snapping everyone's head back. At that same instant, he cocked his right arm over by his left shoulder and then straightened it out, swinging his fist as hard as he could into Rotten Breath's throat, smashing his larynx.

Tony's foot groped for the brake pedal, found it, and he stomped hard, throwing them all forward. Rotten Breath was so disabled from Tony's blow to his throat that when his head bashed the dashboard he was down for the count, a helpless, gurgling rag doll.

Tony grabbed his Ruger. Simultaneously, Powder Nose slammed into the back of Tony's seat, and the jolt released one word in Tony's mind: RUN! He threw his door open and dashed across the road. In the corner of his eye he saw the bad guys' car and, ominously, the third black bastard was crouched in a firing position with what looked like a Tech-9!

Tony leaped. A shallow ditch separated the road from a cornfield field. Airborne a brief instant. Jesus! Rounds whizzing by him already. That was a Tech-9! Bouncing, rolling over, keeping his arms around his head for protection. God he hoped his gun worked. He scuttled back to the edge of the road, held the Ruger above his head, fired a round, then another. The Tech-9 stopped chattering. *Yeah baby, I got some firepower, too.* Tony peered over the embankment. Now! He raised in the shooting position and immediately put two rounds into the red car, which the Tech-9 shooter was now hiding behind.

He ran low and forward in the ditch beside the road, then angled off into the cornfield. Another bang, another round zipping over Tony's head. Good, that little punk is shooting high, he thought. Only a few more feet to go. Duck and crouch! This guy's blasting caps left and right!

Tony's sliced belly had reopened, and blood flowed from the cut. But he was alive. The corn dwarfed him. All around and over his head, tassels burst out the tops of the bulging ears. He lurched through the first few rows. Jesus, his stomach hurt; shoulder did, too, although he couldn't figure out why. But his legs were fine, thank God.

Bullets zinged past him, splattering the fat cobs, and he heard the slower bark of a pistol. That meant Powder Nose was up and firing, helping out his buddy. Tony hoped all three weren't blasting away at him. Odds like that would be hard to beat. He really doubted, though, that Rotten Breath was functional. He had fucked that mother-fucker up. Blood kept soaking his jeans. He took his T-shirt off, wadded it up and held it against his belly.

Low, stumbling, diving through the corn. Lurching deeper into the field, leading with his left, protecting his hurt shoulder and the belly-wound by his belt line. Mosquitoes devoured him. Edges of the sharp leaves he plowed past inflicted a thousand tiny cuts. Welts erupted across his arms, face and neck; then sweat stung the welts and cuts covering his body, making them hurt even more.

He knew he had to keep going. They would track him down if they were truly determined to kill him. And that wouldn't be hard. He was leaving a big trail -- bleeding, breaking stalks. He couldn't help it. He'd been drinking all afternoon when he was hijacked, so his blood was pretty thin. Plus, he hadn't gotten around to eating dinner. He was paying for it now. Tony had a horrible thought that all this intense physical exertion would get his intestines riled up and oozing out of his belly. He ran, hoping the slash hadn't gone that deep, clutching the wadded-up shirt tightly over the cut.

"Mutha-fucka, kill yo white ass!" someone screamed, blasting away. But this time the rounds went wide of Tony by about 20 feet. He couldn't believe his luck. He was still in motion, still in play. He stopped for a moment, catching his breath, then began a more controlled furrowing through the stalks, conscious now of not leaving a trail for his assailants to follow.

Tony traversed a few more rows, then stopped to listen. He didn't hear them thrashing after him. Suddenly a semi-automatic began blasting. Tony heard bullets thunking into steel, followed by an explosion lighting the sky. Goodbye, car. Jesus! He hadn't even finished making payments on it! And then:

"Now we comin' after you, white boy!"

But the black dudes had taken too much time loitering around the cars, and Tony knew he'd run fast enough to reach the river before they could catch him. He stopped trekking at right angles through the corn and began walking parallel to the rows, unafraid to leave tracks now. He doubted those lazy bastards would follow him across the river. Tony quickened his pace. Can't quit now, he kept telling himself. And then he was out of the corn, following the sloping ground to the riverbank, where the breeze in the trees made a song compared to the roar his running gun battle with the thugs had produced.

The Platte is more of a stream than a river in places, shallow enough to walk in. Tony fairly plunged into the water. He burned, bled, stung, sweated and ached. It was deliciously cool, as good as he had imagined it would be.

When the water reached his waist he paused, took the Ruger from his pants, dangled it in front of his eyes for a moment, then dropped it, watching the pistol disappear into oblivion. He rather thought he was through with guns now.

Once during the crossing the water came up to his chest and he dog-paddled on his good side, letting the current take him downstream until his feet dragged river bottom and he was able to get up, striding onto the opposite bank and scooping a handful of mud to hold against his stomach and staunch the bleeding. He walked over to an old river tree, its roots half-in, half-out of the soil, and sat back in a hammock of vines, listening carefully

Tony heard nothing but the clear, cool sound of night, and he knew that he could rest a while before he found a way home and started a new life.

Sisters

First they heard a girl giggle, then smelled cigarette smoke drifting through the front window. The four dogs went crazy: the Akita, the old collie, the little lab pup and the pit bull. Beth and Marie herded them to the bathroom and Rama went to the door. "Hello."

"Knock-knock," a man said. "UPS. Gotta package for this address."

"Johnny? Johnny Two Bears?" Rama asked.

"The one-and-only," a whiskey voice replied. Rama opened the door and motioned him into the hallway. He came with a pretty little thing, obviously the source of the giggling.

Johnny was a thin Indian about six feet tall wearing blue jeans, cowboy boots and a ball cap behind which hung a skinny black ponytail. He was at the top of the neighborhood dealing chain with schwag, kind buds, crank, coke, ecstasy or acid, all supposedly from the straight-up Mexican mafia, about whom everyone knew: *Fuck with them and die.* He handed Rama a kilo of marijuana covered with tape and brown plastic wrap.

She was going to be nice and ask him to sit down and visit, but now that she was actually confronted with

Johnny Two Bears and his companion, Rama changed
her mind. The teen-age redhead encircled by his
powerful arm looked like a pretty little jungle bird
about to be swallowed by a boa. Rama smelled liquor
and realized Johnny and his young tufted-cockatiel
were tipsy. She thought the whole thing reeked of
debauchery.

Johnny, on the other hand, was looking around
expectantly, waiting, perhaps, for a cold beer invitation
or at least a few moments of conversation. After all,
he'd been cooped up in prison for a decade. He liked to
get out and talk to the ladies.

Rama wouldn't bite. "Well," she said. "Good. I'm
sure the guys will call you soon."

He caught on to her, and a cloud crossed his face.
"Oh, yeah, you can count on it," Johnny said.

Just then Beth and Marie returned from securing
the dogs. "Ladies . . . " he leered, lighting up again.
"Good afternoon," and his eyes trolled slowly over
Beth and Marie's bodies before settling on Marie's
ample breasts.

"Can you believe that?" Beth exclaimed after they
left. "The way he was looking at us? Geez, wouldn't be
surprised to see him crawling through the window one
night."

Rama went to her baby on the couch. Jacob was
awake from the commotion, and it did Rama good to
hold something sweet and precious after seeing
something so sleazy.

"That's why we got dogs," Marie replied to Beth.
"To give us a running start."

"What was he over here for, anyway?" Beth asked.

"Well," Rama said. "Apparently Brett made a deal with him, and Aaron and Steve are in on it."

"Brett made the deal?" Beth asked. Brett had just gotten off probation for getting busted last year with possession-under-an-ounce, plus paraphernalia. Beth didn't mind him smoking, but she definitely didn't want him dealing.

Rama nodded her head yes -- it was Brett's deal.

"I'll get us all some tea," Marie said, and returned to the front room in a while with the glasses. "Well," she said, setting them down, "I hope the guys didn't lose their lunch."

"What do you mean? Why would they throw up?" Beth asked. "I thought they went to Chris' to pull some tubes and drink a few beers -- the usual stuff."

"Oh, they didn't tell you?" Marie replied. "You know Chris' two iguanas, Dica and Tiva? Now there should be only one. That was the whole deal of them going over there: drive to the edge of town, shoot Dica, go back to Chris' and eat it. Chris grew up hunting, so killing, skinning, cleaning and cooking a critter's no big deal to him."

"Yeah, but one of his iguanas? Didn't he raise them from tiny little things to three-footers? Hasn't he had them three years or so now?"

"Uh-huh," Marie added as she finished braiding a necklace. "But he always said he bought two iguanas because he was going to raise one and eat it."

Beth shook her head. "I can't believe it," she said.

"I'm with you," Rama replied. "You won't see me over there eating it."

"How are they going to fix it?" Beth asked out of curiosity.

"I don't know," Marie said, holding the necklace up to her throat. "Like it?" she asked. Marie's choker featured green-and-black polished stones set in hemp twine.

Rama nodded approval, then replied to Beth: "Steak it out; bread it, fry it. I don't know."

"Oh my God," Beth said. She saw an image of a knife slicing the iguana's spine and the wet slabs of meat chunking off like salmon steaks. "Why do guys do stuff like that?" she asked. "Can anyone just tell me?"

She looked at the dogs, Asia, Marley, Ivan and Miss Bodacious. The first three slept, but Miss Bodie, a brindled pit with snow on her chest and liquid brown eyes stared at Beth with the love look and the very thought of killing creatures repelled her.

"What can I say?" Rama replied. "The male species is different from us. Ever notice?"

"Yeah, but -- "

"Okay, look," Marie interrupted. "Turn on the TV. Go to the nature channel. Watch the way males tear things up -- mainly each other; you know, the territorial thing and all. And the females? They're taking care of business. Actually, I think guys got screwed. They miss out on a lot of good emotional stuff."

"Snakes and snails and puppy dog tails," Rama said, quoting a nursery rhyme, "that's what little boys are made of," to which Beth added: "And beer and whiskey and promises," bringing laughter from all of them.

"No really. Why do we put up with men?" Beth asked when the giggling had stopped.

"Oh, duh," Marie said. "Like we got any choice -- unless you want to be gay."

"Well," Rama said. "The crazy thing is, they wonder the same thing -- how they put up with us."

"Shoot, we women are easy," Beth said.

"Yeah, right," Rama laughed. Jacob had finished breast-feeding, and she wiped his mouth and hoisted him up to her eyes: "Oh Jacob. You are going to be a good man, do you hear me? A good man." Rama and Aaron were both 26, not married but planning on it soon now that they had Jacob. Rama was all about astrology, reincarnation, chakras and reiki.

The fan breeze ruffled the feathers in her silver-and-turquoise earrings and she brushed a stray dreadlock from her eyes. "Maybe we can look at it this way," she said. "The Hindus have Brahma, god of creation; Vishnu, the preserver; and Shiva, goddess of destruction and reproduction. So they view life in terms of creation, maintenance, and destruction.

"And if you think about it like that," she continued, "Women are the lucky ones because we get to be both creators and maintainers. Guys just seem to destroy stuff a lot." She laughed when she said it to let Beth and Marie know she was speaking somewhat tongue in cheek.

"How about waiting?" Beth asked. "Women need a goddess to symbolize all the waiting we all do." She threaded a draw-string around the throat of a pipe-protector for glass pieces. "That's what women do: we wait for our men, whether they are doing time, off in war or out at night up to no good. Either way you cut it, women wait. We're supposed to be the patient, virtuous ones. It sucks." As if to underscore Beth's frustration the old front window suddenly slid down and slammed into the sill, scaring everyone.

"Look at how much energy you're putting out," Rama said. The big room just to the right of the front door was the work and hobby room where, in their spare time, the three made crafts to sell on consignment at area head shops. It was old, tall-ceilinged and filled with hanging plants--a jumble of emotions and passions; a place of talk, toys, kisses, laughter and music. Colors from corduroy, denim, ribbons, cloth and felt lay splashed about like paint, and by the front window, Beth's prized possession: her sewing machine.

Opposite that, Rama's rocking chair, the one her mother was rocked in as a baby, and her mother before her. And now it was her turn. She felt it in her bones when she rocked Jacob, felt herself connecting with her female ancestors, so strongly sometimes it was as if they were in the room with her. She looked up from Jacob.

"You sound like you'd like to be out there with them," she replied to Beth, keeping the conversation going in a lazy kind of way. "Is that what you want? To be out there running with the guys? Running with the bulls?"

Suddenly Beth pricked her finger with a sewing needle. "Damn!" she exclaimed. "See what you made me do?" A moment later she took her finger out of her mouth. "No, it's not that," she continued.

"Then what?" Rama asked.

Beth's brow creased and her mouth turned downward. "Okay. It's like this. Guys seem so self-centered. It's always what *they* want to do. They don't seem to think about others as long as they're getting their way. So we have to be the patient ones; playing the waiting game. When I know Brett's going to be out for hours, I can't really plan on doing something else. I get a little tired of it."

"Whew!" Marie exclaimed, setting down the necklace she was beading. "Woman with an attitude. You go girl!" She pumped a clenched fist in the air.

"You mean this isn't enough 'fun' for you?" she asked Beth. "Being here . . . with us? Hangin' out wit da goils."

"You know it's not that, Marie. I just get angry at how guys stretch the truth, like: 'I'll be back in just an hour,' or 'I only had a few beers' -- now that's a classic. Then they're gone half the night and come home drunk when before they left they said they didn't want to come home late and drunk."

Rama was burping Jacob and the phone rang. "Well . . . no one threw up," she said after she talked with Aaron. "He said lunch went fine."

"What did he say the iguana tasted like?" Marie asked.

"Chicken, of course," Rama replied. "He said it tasted just like chicken."

"And they all ate it?"

"Uh huh."

"Guys," Beth said. "I just can't figure them out." A few minutes later she was upstairs talking on the phone.

"Do you think she called Brett?" Marie asked.

Rama shrugged. "I hope not. Those two need some distance right now, some cooling-off time." But from the sounds of the conversation Beth was talking to either Brett or her parents. Rama and Marie heard her cry out more than once in frustration.

Soon the stairs creaked under her steps, and when she came into the room it was obvious Beth was upset. She stood at the window, her eyes fighting tears, staring away from Rama and Marie trying to dam her emotions. A police car drove by.

"Oh, great," she said. "A cop. The day keeps getting better and better." She peered out the window until the cop was gone. Then she turned. "Let's see if we can figure this out. A major dealer drops off a kilo of marijuana and within minutes the police drive by. Anyone nervous yet?"

Her words hung in the air. Marie and Rama considered them. Then Marie spoke. "Would you relax?" she implored. "Cops drive by all the time."

In their edgy neighborhood it was good to see an occasional police car, especially when the gang-bangers were mowing each other down. Gunfire was frequently heard at night, as well as the police helicopter beating the air while hovering overhead. Burglars and rapists were frequent, too. People had guns for protection. Marie walked over to Beth and began kneading her shoulders and consoling her.

Marie had no fear of cops, no fear of anything, for that matter. She worked at a bar that was more rough than easy and had no problem charming dollars out of men's billfolds with sexy smiles and strong pours. "Feeling better?" she asked, pushing on a knot in Beth's right shoulder with her thumb. "Geez, you're tight. You gotta loosen up, girl."

"Just seeing cops makes me nervous. I don't know why, I can't help it."

"Relax," Rama urged. "We need to think positively here. This could all be random stuff. To make anything more of it may be foolish."

Beth concentrated on sensation. At first her shoulder muscles hurt from the pressure of Marie's fingers, but eventually she was able to relax. "Oh yeah," she moaned, slowly rolling her head back and forth, side-to-side. "Don't stop now." Tension fell off her shoulders then. Joni Mitchell music was playing and Beth drifted in the massage, thinking of Brett, her silly lover-boy Brett.

She had been going with Brett for a year. Six months ago he moved in the house to share her bed and even more of her life. Her parents met him last Christmas when they flew in for the holidays. Her father didn't like him. "All hot air," he said.

"Is he really reliable in the long run?" added her mother.

In fact, they left Beth a standing invitation to fly back to Denver anytime she wanted -- alone. For one thing, her mom and dad couldn't stand her dreadlocks, which they blamed on him. (Actually, Beth had begun growing her dreads at the same time as Rama.)

Describing why she liked Brett was not easy for Beth. He wasn't particularly cute, smart, or sexy. "He's just Brett," she would say, and shrug. She actually didn't know why she like him. She just did.

Poor Brett. Such good intentions, such little resolve. He tried growing his first ganja crop in the basement last year. Halfway through, mites and mold covered his plants. He spent a small fortune on sprays and pesticides, but the limp marijuana plants were indifferent to his revival attempts. It was as if they did not want to be saved. Then, in a final act of rebellion, one of them morphed, quietly, in the corner, and before Brett realized what was going on the whole garden had seeded: nine, 3-foot-tall, dirt-grown Willies; green as emeralds in their youth, fresh as the breath of life itself.

No one wanted to buy a bunch of seeds, so the guys waited for the colas to dry and then deseeded them, rubbing them between their palms onto baking sheets tilted downward for the seeds to roll off into the trash, and the crystal shake staying behind; scraping away the remaining seeds and stems and twigs. Spending countless hours. And the end-product? Up in smoke of course -- nothing to show for their efforts.

Brett's stock plummeted worse than the Dow in a nosedive. The women considered growing a terrible waste of time and money and a grave danger to the family unit. Moreover, Aaron and Steve were unhappy because Brett had promised them huge buds covered with crystals, and all they saw was mite-infected leaves covered with mold. Even now Brett was trying to make amends with another crop, but the ganja was yellowing badly late in flowering and everyone was beginning to think his thumb was rotten, not green.

After her shoulder massage Beth read Jacob a story about a little red squirrel who kept trying to make a life for herself in spite of interference from gray squirrels.

They guys came home as she finished. They were feeling good, laughing, boasting about eating the iguana. Brett looked at Beth warily. "Are we okay, babe?" he asked. She nodded reluctantly.

Marie looked at Steve and grinned: "C'mere and give momma a kiss, iguana breath." Then all seven of them plus the dogs were in the room now and Rama thought how much of a good family feeling it was. She tried to get several conversations going, asking the guys about dinner, but they shrugged off the question and soon went upstairs to play with their new kilo of marijuana.

And once again the gals were waiting on the guys.

"Whoopee, they're home finally," Beth said. "We're having some fun now."

"They're probably gonna go back out," Marie added.

Rama didn't want to let them bait her into joining the conversation because she was working on controlling her own anger. *Don't go there, Fools rush in where angels fear to tread.* And then, for good measure and just to be sure, she told Jacob: "Fools rush in where angels fear to tread, did you know that, sweetheart?" adding, "Don't you ever let your momma catch you doing that."

Then she waited for what she thought was a reasonable amount of time and went upstairs, knocking on Steve's door and opening it. Aaron was helping Steve make-up and weigh one-ounce bags of the marijuana. Brett was talking on the cordless. Rama wiggled her finger at Aaron.

"A kilo's a bit much, isn't it?" she said to him in the hallway. "Did you know a cop car cruised by shortly after Johnny Two Bears left?"

"No way." Genuine alarm showed in his eyes.

"Yes." She stood resolutely, hands on hips. "So you're getting dope on front from Johnny Two Bears? I know you guys don't have the cash for a kilo." Aaron nodded yes, saw that it wouldn't be enough for Rama. "Johnny called over to Chris' while we there and Brett set this deal up," he explained, adding that they could probably move all the weed tonight, the town had been so dry. It was understood the guys would have to go somewhere else to sling the weed. After Jacob was born, everyone had agreed that no dealing would go on in the house. Personal consumption, yes; but sales were to be done elsewhere.

She still wasn't convinced. "Aaron, do we really need to do this?"

"A thousand dollars profit in a few days," he said, "for doing your friends a favor -- supplying them with weed. Money they're going to spend somewhere on it anyway. How do you say no to that?"

He had her there. Between them, their minimum wage jobs hardly covered the bills. Rama hated it that they had to deal occasionally to make ends meet. It's not that she minded being part of ganja dealing. She was simply concerned about the potential prison time under mandatory-sentencing laws; in short, she could not bear the thought of Aaron in jail. Not Aaron. Jail would crush him.

Marie came up and joined them and watched Brett and Steve break the kilo down and weigh it into ounces of marijuana. Steve kept glancing from the bags of buds to Marie, scanning for signs of anger, but she seemed okay. So many girls did powder where she worked that she figured if all her man did was smoke dope that was fine with her.

"Where's Beth?" Brett asked.

"You need to talk to her," Rama said, emphasizing the word *need*.

Brett shrugged, trudged downstairs with a sigh, and soon the argument that had flared earlier on the phone was roaring again.

Even from upstairs, Rama heard parts of phrases Beth yelled: *Dealing while on probation . . . Skipped dinner . . . Didn't call.*

Then finally: "You don't care how I feel!"

Aaron and Rama had been looking at each other and listening to Brett and Beth. "Aaron," she said, "go down there and break those two up. Maybe it'll look different to them in the morning."

He and Steve broke up the fight by grabbing Brett and dragging him out the door, saying they'd be home around midnight. Beth microwaved popcorn from the kitchen, and it went off with the same angry sounds she'd just showered Brett with, like a drive-by. Rama and Marie looked at each other in the front room, the mutual concern for Beth evident on their faces. Beth, oddly, could not stop filling the house with intense energy today, and it baffled them. The last year-and-a-half of living with Beth -- a sweet, sensitive Pisces -- had truly been trouble-free. Rama and Beth had liked each other from the moment they met.

Beth brought the popcorn into the sewing room and Rama put a Disney video in for Jacob. Soon he was asleep, but the women watched it anyway, talking quietly. Rama rocked and discussed astrology with Beth, who was balancing her checkbook. Beth and Brett were water and fire; she a Pisces, he an Aries. A risk-avoider with a risk-taker. Not the best match. Of course, Rama didn't say it like that.

Marie stood and yawned at a little past 10 o'clock: "That's it, I'm outta here," she said, kissing Jacob on the forehead and saying her goodnights before heading upstairs. Rama and Beth read and listened to Joni Mitchell on low and soon midnight rolled around.

Beth looked at the clock for the hundredth time that night and said "Here we are again. They said they'd be home by now, but here we are, waiting." She rose, wordless, and strode upstairs, trailing unhappiness in her wake. Rama held Jacob and rocked, listening to the clock tick, wondering what the years would bring. She was dozing when she heard something metallic fall upstairs in the bathroom. Scissors? She went to investigate.

"Oh Beth," she said, opening the bathroom door, seeing the pile of dreadlocks on the floor, Beth sitting on the edge of the tub crying. "Are you sure? Did you really want to do that?"

"Color me gone," she sniffed. "Dreads gone, Beth gone." She tried looking up, but it was no good: her face returned to her hands. Rama walked over and held Beth's head against her stomach. "Now, now," she said. "Stay on top of your emotions."

"I know," Beth said. "I just wanted me and Brett to work. We're just not going to."

"Square pegs and round holes," Rama replied. "Never were meant to match."

Beth stopped crying. "How do you stay with Aaron and make it work?"

Rama thought. "It's hard to explain. I'm not sure what he sees in me, but I think he's a pretty neat human being. He makes me want to shine for him. Does that make sense?

Beth nodded yes and stared at the faded blue tiles on the wall. "Brett and I don't love each other," she said. "Not like you and Aaron do. So . . . I . . . decided to go back to Denver."

"Oh Beth," Rama said again. "I'm sorry." Rama felt helpless. What could she say? She hugged Beth and after a while she stopped crying and Rama looked into her eyes. "Well, let's get you finished up for the next chapter of your life, sister," she said, picking the scissors up and cutting the rest of Beth's hair, handing the shorn dreads to her one-by-one. Beth gathered them in her lap, staring at them with all the solemnity of a mourner at a funeral.

A door closes and a door opens, Rama thought, clipping the last dreadlock and giving Beth a final hug. "Now wash your hair and I'll cut it again tomorrow to even it out. I need to check on Jacob."

He was the picture of peace in his playpen downstairs. She stared at her son for a long time, Jacob, hair coal-black like his father's and, already, a merry little laugh. She looked and the clock read 1:30.

Where in the hell were the guys?

Anger rose up in her like smoke from a distant valley. She felt the slow burn, the first few flames crackle to life, and she reminded herself not to go there. She lit a candle and an incense stick and sat down in her mother's, grandmother's and great-grandmother's rocker, resting her hands on the wooden arms worn smooth by ceaseless hours of women waiting and worrying for their men and children.

Rama would talk to Aaron in the morning, or whenever his head cleared. He would be remorseful, mope around for days afterwards, disappointed in himself. She, meanwhile, prayed for patience. She created a picture of Aaron in her mind and surrounded it with white light.

Then Ivan, the lab pup, waddled in with his tail wagging, and she lifted him to her lap where he curled up and went to sleep as she rocked and waited for the guys to come home. A Joni Mitchell song about a woman who loved her man was playing, and Rama gathered the notes up in her head and sent them flying out the window to go find Aaron and bring him home.

Bus Bust

*That crazy cop was trying to pull the whole frickin'
bus over!*

Sean heard the siren, snapped his head up and saw the lights flashing alongside the bus. "Jesus," he said, "What's their problem?" But the unmarked cruiser wouldn't pass, and then it dawned on him. That crazy cop wants the bus to stop!

"Look at this," Sean said, nudging Jeff. Jeff was already awake and staring, too tired to say anything. Sean glanced back at Kevin. He was passed-out, head back, mouth open. Kevin had almost gotten thrown off the bus a few hours ago with a wino he was slamming 40-ouncers with.

Sean wondered if the driver had been speeding. *Why else would cops pull a bus over?*

The cops were on board in a moment, two medium-size guys in blue jeans, one a little older than the other, 40 maybe. Fancy tennis shoes, athletic builds, short-sleeve polo shirts. Didn't really look like cops until the first one -- mustache, hair starting to gray -- brandished his badge at arm's length, panning it back and forth slowly, the fat silver star against black leather.

"Nevada State Narcotics Division," he said. "We have reason to believe that a shipment of drugs is aboard this vehicle. If you are not carrying drugs, you have nothing to worry about. If you are, we advise you to give yourself up now. It will only go easier on you in a court of law." As he spoke, he walked slowly down the aisle, stopped about halfway -- right by Sean -- and stared into his eyes.

Jesus Mary, Mother-of-God, he thought, the adrenaline going off in him like Fourth of July bottle rockets, the same feeling he had the first time he got pulled over: red-and-blue cherries exploding in his rearview mirror, police siren splitting his ears and a blade of fear slicing with the realization that he was holding some pot and the cops would throw his ass in jail if they found it. Straight up, no kidding

Yeah, that was the feeling, all right. And once again, here he was holding some pot and staring frozenly, along with everyone else on the bus, at the Nevada Narco-Cop. *The trick is to look calm,* he reminded himself. *Look calm even though you are freaking out inside*. Blood pounded his temples. The air was electrical with anticipation and fear, and Sean swore he heard atoms crackling and colliding. He struggled to make his breath regular. *Sweet Jesus, how did he get in these situations?*

The trip was weird from the beginning. The first night out three weeks ago, when they still had a car, they stopped for the night at a state park in Montana. Kevin opened his coat to give Ike and Izzy, his ganja iguanas, some fresh air. The lizards had been lounging under his armpits and napping against his chest since sunset, their once bright-green skin darkening however, to a troublesome brown. Izzy in particular looked pooped; his dorsal crest of soft spines lay flat against his body and he could barely keep his thin eyelids at half-mast.

Then the reptiles shocked everyone when they leapt to the ground and scurried off for a new life into the inky night of the April prairie, which, considering that iguanas are tropical lizards, was going to be decidedly short.

Kevin was distraught, running all over the place, calling their names, begging them to return, making them promises everyone knew he wouldn't keep: fresh water always, constant Rasta beats, ganja leaves 24-7. But it was no use. The iguanas were gone.

Not a good omen, they decided. Not a good omen at all.

Of course, Deb was still holding up well at that point. She didn't give two hoots about the freakin lizards anyway. Her cheeks were fairly burning from the excitement that comes at the beginning of journeys, when hope runs high and the miles yet untraveled beckon like presents waiting to be opened. No, Deb, along with her car, would not come apart until later -- in San Francisco.

Sean returned the Narco-Cop's stare, realizing the bastard was micro-analyzing him: pupil dilation, sweat, rapid pulse, shallow breathing. Then a flash of activity outside and a third police officer pulled up in a truck and came out putting a leash on a black German Shepherd. Sean was glad the Narco-Cop turned around and walked back up by the driver, but still, his face fell big-time seeing the dog.

That's it, he thought. *I'm a dead duck*. He had a quarter-ounce of kind buds hidden inside his backpack in the overhead compartment. He could maybe get that past a cop--but a friggin drug dog? Holy Cow. His stomach headed south and went all queasy, followed by his thoughts, which turned regretful. *Why oh why did he have to smoke dope? Nevada. Let's see. A no-tolerance state. Everything a felony. A seed, a pipe, a roach, a bud. A felony.* More fear, more regret, more remorse.

Sean looked at Jeff. He had about five or six seeds. The object was to get those seeds back home and grow them. It was a good plan, a plan that could work. But now, as usual, the cops were trying to fuck it up. Always trying to ruin your day, Sean thought. He doubted Jeff would be in trouble even if the cops did find his seeds. But he had no doubt that they would be very upset to find his six or seven grams of buds. Oh, man, if a joint was a felony, what the hell was a quarter-ounce -- a life sentence in the slammer with all the hard-core criminals?

Jeff had found the bag yesterday talking to a couple guys in line at the grocery store. One thing led to another, and they all ended up getting stoned together. Turns out they happened to have a couple of sacks for sale, so Jeff and Sean split one.

Jeff was like that. He would ride a whim or bet on a hunch in a second, which was odd for a guy who usually did nothing, for he had long periods of inactivity sitting around his mother's house due to a loathing for work and affinity for LSD. A great slacker, he and Sean met in high school through a mutual interest in marijuana and skipping school to smoke it. By graduation, they were fast friends. Now they could only stare at each other.

"What the fuck," Jeff muttered. "A dog?" His brow furrowed in consternation.

A murmur rose throughout the bus as the door whooshed open and the third man bounded up the steps behind the lunging beast, a great, black thing that flashed incisors, uttered growls and barked three times quickly: Whuff! Whuff! Whuff! like a gun going off, then snarled a foot or two away from the nearest passengers' faces. People were terrified. Everyone froze in place harder than ice-cubes in a tray while the dog-handler held firm to the beast on the leash, his forearm muscles clenching. The cop was a commando. His head was clean-shaven, he was outfitted in black weapons and chest gear, and wore combat boots.

GI Joe, just like the friggin' movies, Sean thought.

Total silence for a second; shock, disbelief, everyone staring. Then a baby up front let loose a shrill scream, and from the way her screeching sounded there was a lot more water behind that dam. Murmuring swept the bus. From the rear, cursing. "Fucking cops!" "Pigs!" These were people who knew the feel of a lawman's boot on the back of their necks or the sound of a judge's gavel sentencing them to jail, taking what little money they had. No friends of the cops here.

Sean shook his head and let it hang, his eyes following the black rubber mat running the length of the bus, back toward Kevin. Good ol' Kevin, awake now, of course. Their eyes locked. Kevin held out his palms in a shrug.

"Quiet down! the tall cop shouted. "Quiet down right now!" He shot a glance at the driver, who, taking a cue, cut the engine. The bus stopped shuddering. "OK, let's go," the K-9 commando said to the driver, who followed him outside. Then the older narc shut the door and turned to face the passengers.

"Please stay where you are," he commanded. "My partner and I are going to visit with each and every one of you individually. To facilitate the process, please have your driver's license or some other form of I.D. available. Avoid sudden moves. If you need to reach your overhead luggage, please wait until we get to you to do so."

The narc looked to the back of the bus. "Yes, ma'am," he said.

"Yes, uhm, may I please be excused to use the ladies room?" came a sweet-sounding little-girl voice.

Sean knew who that was. She had to be the bleach blonde sitting with the guy who looked like a meth freak, although earlier he'd told Kevin that he was a Marine on leave from the San Diego Recruit Depot, and Kevin had thought: *Right, and I'm a famous heart surgeon.* Even though the "Marine" and his lady had just met, the pangs of love or lust -- or both -- had risen as quickly as the sun went down. Kevin, who sat opposite them in the aisle and therefore a little closer to the action, told Sean that the amorous duo spent half the night in the tiny bathroom making all types of carnal noises, converting the john into a miniature X-rated movie set reeking of sweat, sex, food, cigarettes and liquor.

Sean smiled when the officer told her she'd have to wait, but then she asked, "Wait for what? 'Cause no one's gonna search me," at which point all the men on the bus busted out laughing. Now everyone turned and stared at the raggedy couple. Crumbs of white powder had fallen out of the boyfriend's nose and mixed in his mustache. Looked like he tried to gobble up as much of his stash as he could and did a pretty thorough job of it.

The baby was screaming really good and steady now. Its cries joining the racket as shouts of indignation rang out from young and old passengers alike while others, still, began making requests of the lawmen. In other words, complete mayhem. That's it, Sean thought. I'm trapped in hell. And then he caught himself. No, hell is where you're going if you get busted.

He felt a small shake as the driver opened a luggage panel below and the support arms locked in place. The wolf-dog began barking again and everyone quieted, listening to the growling and yapping, the suitcases and bags being dragged out, the K-9 cop encouraging it: "Go, Bojo, go! Find the dope, Bojo! Find the dope!"

Jeff snickered. "Bojo. What a stupid name."

Sean smiled and nodded at Jeff. His long black hair covered the top half of his Grateful Dead tie-dye, and the bright orange shirt hung over dirty jeans and tennis shoes that had seen better days. "I'd like to get that dog in my house," Sean whispered to him. "I've got all kinds of nugs I've lost over the months he could find for me."

Meanwhile, the two Nevada Narco-boys worked their way toward Jeff and Sean in the middle of the bus. The cops didn't seem to spend much time with the passengers up front. As the cops neared Sean and Jeff, they stopped whispering to each other. No point in Jeff being associated with Sean if he got busted. The Lone Ranger strategy.

The Narco-Cops were two seats away, asking passengers for the copy of their bus ticket. In front of Sean sat an old black gent with a cane and a middle-aged white woman whose New England Yankee accent had been driving Sean crazy. He wondered if the officers were in a hurry to get to Jeff, and sure enough, they did go for him first.

"Bus ticket and driver's license, please," the older cop said.

Jeff withdrew his billfold and opened it. Right in the middle was the folded slip of paper with the seeds. He tried to get his hand over it while drawing out his driver's license, but the younger cop saw it.

"What's in the paper?" he asked, holding out his hand.

"Nothing," Jeff stammered, "s-some addresses."

The cop grabbed it and opened it, and there they were, seven plump little seeds. "I wonder what kind of seeds these are?

"I'm not really sure myself. Someone just gave 'em to me a few days ago. Said to take 'em home and grow them."

"You didn't want them, though, did you?" he asked.

Jeff held up his hands. "No, not at all, go ahead."

"Good answer," he said, and with that, the cop with the mustache turned his attention to Sean.

The trick is to look calm, Sean reminded himself. He tried to pretend the quarter-ounce of kind buds wasn't overhead, just an arm's reach away, but his recent diet of coke, coffee and candy bars had left his nerves bare, and he just didn't know if he could pull it all off. He felt like he was on the edge of something really bad maybe, like in a movie where the plot veers horribly off-course.

"I.D."

"It's overhead, in my backpack."

The cop jerked his head upward. "Get it."

Sean got the bag down, opened it, got his billfold, pulled out his license and bus ticket and handed them to the cop, grateful that his hand wasn't shaking. He thought of the scene in Star Wars when Obi Wan Kenobi sent the mind-signal to the Imperial troopers stopping them: *"These aren't the droids you're looking for."* Sean tried that now, facing the plain-clothes cop. *We're not the people you're looking for*, he thought, practicing his best Jedi mind control on the narc. *We're not the people you're looking for.*

"Where ya headed?"

"Home, to be with my family for Easter."

"What else is in there?" the cop said, eyeing the colorful corduroy fabric.

"Here, I'll show you," he said, starting to pull stuff out. "A water bottle, my cigarettes, packa gum, lighter, a candy bar, my pager . . . "

"Pager!" he shot back. "You in a gang at home?"

"No. My mom got it for me for this trip," Sean lied. "She says that way, she'll start to worry if she pages me and doesn't hear from me in 12 hours."

Their eyes met, but just then Bojo went berserk outside. Everyone could hear the silly, misinformed dog barking his throat out. Like any mutt, he was probably working for treats and his master's praise. Sean wished he could light a big hooter and blow smoke in Bojo's face -- mellow that dog right out.

Everyone stared outside. The K-9 cop and the driver each dragged out big, green suitcases from the cargo bay. The dog bolted over and began tearing at the bags, going nuts. The cop plunged a knife into one of the suitcases, ran it around the edge and ripped back the big flap of cloth, and -- hubba-bubba, wouldja lookat that? -- The mother lode, a serious smoking stash. The other bag, same thing. Two big Samsonites full of pressed Mexican brickweed, dark green, dry. Maybe a hundred pounds.

And then it hit Sean. The cops weren't doing a random little nickel-and-dime drug bust. They must have known about this load all along -- a tip-off or something. In short, he was free. The fuzz had what they wanted, and hallelujah, it wasn't him!

The K-9 cop was on the bus in an instant. Holding his arm out, he dangled the yellow shipping tags from the suitcase. "Okay, I got a free ticket for a one-way trip to the state penn for the passenger going to Philadelphia," he said.

No one moved. No one made a noise.

"C'mon people. Humor me here. I said, who's going to Phil-a-del-phia?"

Commotion from the back, someone saying no, the voice getting louder and louder. *"No soy culpable, no soy culpable,"* came the choked sound. I am not guilty. It was the Latino. Sean remembered him playing pinball at the bus depot in Reno. And then the cuffs came out, but the prisoner-to-be wouldn't get in them, so the K-9 cop went after him like a wrestler, hooking his knee, grabbing his arms, wrenching them behind his back and clicking the steel traps shut across his thin wrists. The poor fellow knew the game was up. He quit struggling and lay still, his lips moving in silent prayer, and he was lifted and hauled off the bus, a trapped rabbit.

The older narc stood by the door: "Thanks for the cooperation, everyone. Sorry for the inconvenience. Have a nice day."

And then they were gone. The driver cranked the engine, shifted into gear and pulled onto the highway. A moment later they were rolling down the road, everyone still in shock. But the sense of relief was palpable, something they could almost touch or feel in the air. Life was suddenly fresh again, offered hope once more.

Jeff looked at Sean. "Dude, did we dream that or what?"

" I don't know but I'll tell you what," Sean replied. "This is the last damn time I ever take a bus."

Finders Keepers

There's precious little compensation in this world, and you gotta take it where you find it.

Stephen saw her first.

He had just changed the oil on the sheriff's cruiser, and now he was doing his own improvements. He slid a safety pin into the rubber brake-line hose overhead, then withdrew it and looked at the pinprick with a smile. In a few days that one drop would become a drip, then a trickle; then the trickle would become a gusher and the gusher would burst, spewing brake fluid all over God's creation -- maybe strand the cop while he was chasing a drug dealer.

And if that didn't sideline the cop, maybe a loose bolt on the cruiser's rear end would do the trick. Stephen hated him some cops, and he took great joy in fucking up their cars whenever he could. They had busted him for so many things the last few years (possession-under-an-ounce, twice; drug paraphernalia, driving under the influence; minor in possession of alcohol) that he was always glad to repay the favor.

In fact, getting even with all the county sheriffs and state troopers who brought their hotrods to AOK Carwash was the only part of his job he truly enjoyed.

He was looking for a wrench when sunlight bouncing off chrome temporarily blinded him. From his underground lair -- the oil pit -- he poked his nose up to ground level, and there she went, gliding past in a red Corvette like a comet, gold hair blowing in the breeze, gold bracelets glinting on bronze arms. A rich man's wife. Stephen whistled lowly and slowly. *One night*, he thought. *One night with a woman like that.*

Then a piece of debris fell onto his face from the sheriff's cruiser and he wiped at it with a greasy hand, smearing his cheek. "Where's that goddamn wrench," he muttered to himself.

Paul saw her next.

He and Ian were standing at the entrance to vacuum bay No. 1. "Gonna be hot," Ian said dejectedly. "You watch. Ninety or more. There's not a cloud in the sky. The whole damn town's gonna want their cars washed."

Paul stared at the pavement, head bowed, numb with the weight of knowing that he would have to clean hundreds of cars before he trudged home covered in sweat hours from now.

"Dude," he said, "I'm wasted. I don't wanna work."

As usual, Paul was running on empty. His band played a bar gig last night and, Ian recalled when he left at midnight, Paul was tossing shots of Jack Daniels. Paul could party all night and work all day like no one Ian had ever seen.

"I hate this job," Paul said. "Just hate it."

"That makes two of us" Ian replied. "But what are you gonna do?"

Paul scratched his just-shaved cheek, irritated at the inconvenience of having to be clean-cut for a lousy carwash job. "I need to get high in the worst kind of way," he mumbled.

Ian nodded. "Didn't you catch one last night with those chicks who had some kind buds?"

"Yeah, but that was last night. I'm talking about now."

Then Paul peered beyond Ian's shoulder. "Oh my God," he whispered. "Would you get a load of that!"

Ian turned just in time to see the Corvette purr up to a stop at their station: the vacuum bay where it all began, the entry point to the multimillion dollar car wash empire of Mister Arthur Abbot.

The car door opened, and a long brown leg, white sandal, red toe nails, gold ankle bracelet, touched the ground. Ian went into his automatic mode and walked over to the goddess. "Welcome to AOK Car wash, ma'am." He held her door open.

"Hi. Now what?" she asked, honey and wine in her voice. She rose and stood like Venus coming out of the sea.

"I'll take it from here," he said, pointing to the waiting room. "They'll call your name when your car's ready."

As she turned and walked across the shop floor the other guys at work did the "wave," their heads bobbing like the toy dogs on the back windowsills of old cars, looking at the blonde but making it seem like they weren't. Her shorts creased from left to right like windshield wipers under each bun when she walked --

blink, blink; blink, blink, temporarily freezing the all-male crew in place like Medusa herself.

Jess broke the spell. "Okay, okay," he boomed, "Let's get back to work 'fo ya'll throw your necks out." And he chuckled, "Sho 'nuf a good-lookin' woman; yessir, a mighty fine, good-lookin' woman."

"Yeah, you know she got her a sugar daddy," Ian grinned. What a chick. Her Vette was quick to vac. "Now look at this," Jess exclaimed, working opposite Ian in the car. Jess held a present about the size of a pen box, its silver wrap laced with red ribbon. Ian smiled and shook his head. "Must be nice," he shouted, "that someone can give you a present, and you're so rich you shove the gift under your car seat and forget about it."

They found the weirdest stuff sometimes. Jess had the most stories to tell since he'd been there so long, almost ten years now. Rumor had it that he'd discovered everything but a corpse in the cars over the years. Technically, anything left behind at the vacuum bay was considered trash. Reminding customers to that effect, signs were posted: "PLEASE . . . Secure All Valuables Before Entering Carwash Bay."

Of course, discretion ruled. Jess set the gift on the dash where the blonde would see it. The guys were deeply suspicious of a trap, for good reason. They worked under constant surveillance. Also, the Abbotts' would occasionally plant a $20 bill or a Crown Royal sack full of quarters in a car and run it through the wash. And you better hope that stuff wasn't in your pockets when the car came out the other end because they would call the cops and have you arrested. But loose change, no problem.

Ian pocketed two quarters he found under the rear floor mat when the security camera up in the corner swiveled its black snout away from him. Some days he made as much as ten bucks by picking up change and an occasional dollar bill. Usually it was a matter of pick the money up or let the vac hose eat it.

They finished the blonde's Vette and Ian drove it over to the million-dollar guts of the beast -- the underground chain system that towed all vehicles through 200 feet of soap, suds, spraying, washing, rinsing and spinning water nozzles.

Next up, a yuppie SUV. The guy pulled in so fast he almost hit Paul with the front of his truck.

"Hey, how long's this gonna take?" he demanded.

"Not long, sir," Paul said. "About ten minutes."

"Okay . . . make sure and get all this dirt off, okay?" he directed, then added: "And by the way, it's pretty dirty inside, too."

Ian felt like saying "That's our job you idiot -- getting the dirt off. Why do you think we're here? And next time you come roaring in to this bay and almost hit my homeboy Paul I'm gonna punch your lights out."

But instead he put on his fake happy-face: "We'll do our best, sir. I think you'll like the results."

Yet he just stood there, his tasseled loafers and perfectly creased slacks an insult to the crew members staring back at him through layers of dirt, grime and sweat. Ian thought the customer looked like someone who watched people work for a living, maybe one of those corporate types who stares out his air-conditioned office window at the shop floor below him, holding a stopwatch to blue-collars workers.

Or maybe he sat up there determining who was going out the door when the next downsizing was announced. Reorganizing departments and work teams was also good sport in order to improve the bottom line. Perhaps he did that.

"Sir, you'll be more comfortable in the air-conditioned waiting room," Ian suggested. The guy thought it over, then left reluctantly. And he was right: his SUV was a pig sty. The floor was concealed beneath a layer of empty coffee cups, soda cans, fast-food wrappers, bottles and junk mail. Even the ashtrays overflowed with cigarette butts. Ian was glad to see a Swiss Army knife under the front seat. The knife was dirty, obviously forgotten. *Freaking yuppie*, Ian thought. *It's mine now*. He pulled the mats, front and back. Hung them, sprayed them.

Cleaning up the trash of the world, that's what they did. Of course they hated their jobs, but they loved them, too, in a perverse kind of way. Where else could they go to work with a hangover and -- if it rained -- get sent home for the day? Or if they woke up and it was raining, not even go in?

Ian walked over to Paul. "Dude, we're screwed," he told him. "No way we'll get time off for lunch today." They cast disgusting looks at the ever-growing line of cars, vans and trucks outside the vac bay. On busy days, subway sandwiches, burgers, or pizza were ordered and the crews had to eat while working -- no clocking out for lunch. That meant Ian and Paul wouldn't be able to smoke their customary bowl of herb, and this stressed them to no end. They figured working for a few hours wasn't too bad if you could count on catching a buzz at the end.

The carwash beast groaned and stretched and rattled and shook. Motors, cables, belts, brushes, pulleys and chains roared and spun, fighting to rid themselves of the automotive intruders, the filthy metallic trespassers. The big gray transformers out back thrummed steadily, sucking megawatts down from the power plant to keep the beast running. The temperature hit 87. Inside, even under the fans, temps hovered in the '90s. Time stood still in a void of sweat. Ian, Paul and the others became lost in labor.

Jess came over. "Ian, take those two clowns and open Number Three." He motioned at two 17-year-old high-school guys punching the time clock. They kept their heads down and did their job without complaining so they were tolerated by older crew members like Ian and Paul who graduated a few years ago. Also, Jess watched out for them because they were varsity wrestlers and he was a near-Olympic caliber wrestler himself.

Ian wiped his brow. His blue work shirt, the AOK logo in yellow-and-red on one side and his name sewn on the other, clung to him already. And, as always, exhaust fumes from the hundreds of cars and trucks seeped into his lungs, making him dizzy and noxious. Christ it was hot. He waved the two guys over and they opened up the remaining bay door. Immediately cars began lining up. Above it all they heard Jess' voice booming.

"All right, all right. Let's make it happen -- get that mojo woikin'. Hit it and git it, boys; hit it and git it."

Legs, backs, forearms straining; knuckles, fingers scraped and cut. No time to stop. Take a look at all the cars, would you? Whatsa matter, crybaby? Little cut on your finger? Gotta go get some first aid, leave me with this frickin' line of cars myself? Thanks a lot, wussie boy. That's it, run to momma. There you go. Just don't come back to me.

"Keep it moving. Don't run, but don't lollygag," Jess shouted above the roar of fans, vacuums, motors and moving equipment. Jess was their first sergeant; they knew he would get them through this, and they followed him. "We got it now," he shouted encouragement. "C'mon . . . Lots of people waiting. Fast and clean, that's what they want. Give 'em what they want. Clean those cars! C'mon, in it to win it! Hump it, jump it, pump it!"

Finally, a lull in the line. They'd beaten down and survived another lunch-hour rush. Guys straightened up and stretched sore lower backs; some took aspirin, amphetamines or energy-booster supplements while others got drinks or washed up. Ian slipped off quickly to the cinder-block bathroom in the vac bay. James was inside, gripping the sink with both hands and leaning into the mirror, staring at his face.

"Dude," Ian said. "What in the hell are you doing? You okay?" James' eyes were thunderously dark and his eyebrows arched angrily.

"Bastards told me to shave or go home," he said.

He stood there thinking about it, staring at the stubble of a three-day goatee--his first ever--and then to the razor and can of shaving cream lying on top of the sink like insults, mocking him, symbolizing the power of lords over serfs. And above the mirror, the words: "No rings. No jewelry. No facial hair. No exceptions."

Ian felt bad for James, but he couldn't do anything about it. He'd been there himself more than once, standing in the same spot with the same decision to make: to shave, or not to shave? Ian finished his business and left silently.

Outside, Bill was waving Jess over. Bill never came to workers; rather, they always came to him. He was a great one for the formality of being the boss, of acting like he was CEO of a multimillion dollar company instead of the Abbots' errand boy. Usually Bill stayed up front by the car wash exit and schmoozed with customers as they waited for the front-end crew to dry their cars.

Jess returned with a grim face. "Ian. Shit's gonna go down. Anyone got anything in their pockets don't belong to 'em, get rid of it. Pass it on."

Ian went over to Paul's crew and warned them of the impending search, then asked, "Where's Paul?"

Out back tossing his cookies, they said.

Then Paul appeared, a little white behind the gills.

"We've been busted," Ian said. "Mr. Abbot and Bill want to search us and our lockers."

"For what?" Paul asked.

"A customer's saying he got ripped off. He called the cops. They're on the way."

"Called the fucking cops. What was in the bag? Diamonds?"

"He's not saying," Ian replied. "But I guess he's awful pissed."

"Oh great," Paul cried. Sweat streamed down his pale face.

"Are you all right," Ian asked.

"Where's the bong?" he chuckled. "One hit and I'll be fine."

"Sure," Ian joked. "It's right out in my car. Open the trunk and find the beer cooler. It's filled with ice, cold beers and a bong loaded with Willies. Ready for a hit? We'll shut the place down and go party."

They vacuumed a few more cars and a soccer mom's filthy minivan with three squabbling brats. A few moments later Ian looked over and saw Bill joined by Mr. Abbot and another person. Mr. Abbot rarely came to the vac bay, the grungiest place in the car wash: freezing in winter, sweltering in summer. The doors were always open due to the exhaust fumes from all the cars and trucks. Large stand-up fans blew the foul air vigorously, and intake vents above sucked it up constantly, but the air was still polluted by hundreds of vehicles a day.

The word went around. Locker search. The crew members came one-by-one in the back room and opened their lockers. Old Man Abbot stood glaring. No one spoke. Ian came in and opened his locker, not bothering to look at Old Man Abbott on the way out. He didn't even know what the bastards were looking for. When all the lockers were open, Bill and Mr. Abbot appeared with the irate customer, and it was the yuppie with the filthy SUV! They toured the lockers.

Their faces were still sour when they emerged a few moments later, however. Bill motioned Jess over, and Jess returned. "Ian, shut down your bay and empty the trash cans."

"Huh? Really? No kidding? Empty the trash cans?"

"Yeah, that's what he's saying."

Each bay had a "trash can," a 50-gallon drum that was the final repository of all the junk sucked up by the vac hose. Ian jabbed in the direction of a drum with his finger. "If we pour all that shit on the floor we're just gonna hafta shovel and sweep it back in again." His voice rose in frustration. "What is so goddamn important for us to be doing this?"

Bill walked up. "Let's go, gentlemen," he snapped.

"Bill . . . Ian began,

Bill interrupted. "Ian, if you want to keep working here, empty the cans now."

Ian felt like he'd just been slapped. His jaw muscles clenched and tightened, and his mouth became a resolute line. He locked eyes with Bill, saw that he was seriousness, went to the first drum and snarled at the two high-school guys. They helped Ian take the top off and shake the hated trash out on the floor. About 30 pounds of dirt, dust, hair, fur balls, pennies, nickels, lifesavers, broken candy, chips, gum, gum wrappers, fast food wrappers, crackers, cookie pieces, hamburger bits, dog food, crumbs and plastic action figures tumbled out.

"Now what?" Ian said.

"We're looking for a plain, brown, paper bag," Bill replied.

A brown paper bag? they replied. What's in it?

"The customer's not saying," Bill replied.

But we're not sifters, they said -- we're throwers and cleaners. It's not our job to evaluate the junk we suck up and toss out -- not when there are 20 or more cars waitin' in line and everyone breathin' down our necks.

Finally Bill relented somewhat. "Awright, awright, take it easy," he said. "Look, for all I know, this guy's a nut, okay? But we gotta do this."

Hey, we're starvin', they said. Are we gonna get lunch today?

No one could figure out how Old Man Abbott got around the law, but he did, year in and year out, mercilessly working young men without breaks or food, working them so hard on some weekends that they would go home at sundown and pass out from exhaustion, many times in the filthy clothes they'd just spent the last eight hours in.

A city cop pulled up in a black-and-white cruiser. The irate customer walked over and began talking to the officer while Old Man Abbot stood at the trash heap. "So help me, Bill," he said. "If one of our guys has done this, I'm gonna . . . I don't know what I'm gonna do. But I can't stand a thief." His face turned from pink to red behind his gold-framed trifocals.

The Abbots were pillars in their church and made a big deal about being Christians, but everyone who worked for them knew what they really worshipped was the Almighty Dollar.

The cop and the irate customer came over. "Sir," he was saying, "It's hard to help you look for something you can't describe."

"I tell you," the customer said, "It's just something in a brown paper sack -- a sack like you'd take your lunch to school in. And the sack was wrapped around the thing that was in it -- something very valuable to me. I don't know what's so hard to explain about that."

"Okay, okay," the cop said. "So let's look." They began poking at the first mound of dirt and junk. Nothing. Old Man Abbot had two high-schoolers procure sticks and poke around the remaining two trash mounds while everyone looked on. Again, nothing. They had turned the fans off to keep the trash from blowing around. Now that the tension was gone from the scene, everyone realized how hot it was. But the customer wasn't quite ready to give up. He paced from one trash pile to the next, then wheeled on some of the guys. "One of you took it, didn't you!" he shouted. They shook their heads no.

Old Man Abbot came up. "Sir," he said. "I don't know what else to do. We have been trying to help, but we just didn't find anything." The cop walked over.

"So you searched the lockers and the trash cans and didn't find it?" he said. "That being the case, I don't know what to tell you. Especially since you can't specifically describe the thing." The cop left.

The customer knew he was beaten. His shoulders slumped and his face fell. Then Stephen appeared. He walked up to the group.

"Mr. Abbot," he said. "The lube shop's been pretty slow, and if it's okay with you, I wouldn't mind giving the customer here a complimentary oil change and lube."

Mr. Abbot's face lit up. "Why thank you, Stephen, that's a very nice offer." He put his arm around

Stephen's shoulder and looked at the irate customer. "Please, sir, it's on the house. Stephen is one of our best employees. He'll be happy to take care of you."

Ian and Paul almost busted out laughing. Paul whispered to Ian: "There goes that guy's brakes."

"Oh, what the hell -- why not?" the customer said.

"Okay guys," Old Man Abbot said. "Get that trash picked up and let's get back to work."

On their way back to the vac bays Paul mentioned to Ian how the customer was such a dick that he deserved to be ripped off.

"Hell yeah, he was a dick," Ian replied. "I just wonder what was in that sack. It had to be something illegal if he wouldn't say what it was."

"Yeah, I don't know what he's griping about. I mean, it's not like he had kind buds or anything."

Ian stopped and grabbed Paul's arm.

"Now how would you know that?" he asked, staring into his eyes..

"Let me put it to you this way," Paul grinned. "Wanna smoke some reefer after work?"

Sticks And Stones

Max had only one chance left before the thing eating his soul drove him stark raving mad.

He was carving himself into madness, one stick at a time, and there was nothing he could do about it.

No more than a week ago, Max's walking canes featured the elaborate designs and ornate etchings he was known for -- dragon faces, castle towers, mountain peaks -- all carved with love and patience. Then, inexplicably, the head of ugliness began rearing from his creations, destroying them, laying waste to the beauty in his wood and in his soul.

Just last night in his workshop he had selected a handsome aspen staff, examined it and decided to fashion a cat's head on the handle-end. Perhaps it would appeal to a feline-fancier, he figured. That was the name of his game: moving product. Three years after graduating from high school and running up and down I-29 and I-70, he had a fledgling business going. Head shops in St. Louis and Columbia, Kansas City and Lawrence, and Omaha and Lincoln sold his canes on consignment. He even got on the web a few months ago, and was waiting for his page to generate some business. Max was making it on his own -- just barely. He loved working with wood, feeling its weight and heft, thinking about its possibilities, carving it, shaping it, bringing out its potential. Wood was a living thing to Max; it connected him to a world of myth and wonder.

He thought about the staff of aspen in his hands, gathered on his most recent trip to New Mexico, and wondered about when it had lived and what it had witnessed. The Zuni? Hopi? Navajo? Buffalo Soldiers? Conquistadors? Perhaps the aspen provided shade to a weary cowboy once, or travelers.

Maybe some unlucky hombre dangled from a rope over one of its limbs. Max sanded and shaped and thought, becoming lost in the creation of his cat-head cane. Yet, when he was almost done, what emerged was not feline at all; rather, it was misshapen and ugly; a snarl forming on its wooden lips; a furrowed brow presiding over its evil eyes.

What the hell! Max thought, staring at the monstrosity, the face of a gargoyle.

Then he heard a scuffling noise amongst the various canes and lengths of sticks against the wall. He peered at them, saw nothing. Animals could be out, he supposed; it was the middle of July. Max walked over to the wood. Suddenly he heard a yowl -- a hellish-sounding yowl -- and a black kitten streaked from the sticks and shot out the garage door. So something had been there! But why would a kitten come in the garage?

Gingerly, Max poked around the upright staffs. When he saw a mash of black feathers and red meat, he realized what was going on. But what he couldn't figure out was how such a little black cat could have caught and eaten such a large bird. It looked like an adult crow. Weird.

He bent over and grabbed the dead bird by the claw
to put it in the trash, but somehow the foot flexed,
driving a talon into the meat of his thumb and drawing
blood. But that wasn't possible. He looked at the bird. It
was in pieces, guts hanging from its body, one wing
gone. In short, the bird was dead. *So how could a dead
bird stick him?*

Max wrapped the crow in newspaper, trashed it and
quit for the night. On the short walk from the garage to
the house, darkness was so complete he tripped, even
though he knew the way, of course, but there was no
moon tonight. Plus, he was distracted by two green
animal eyes staring at him from the far corner of the
yard; not moving, just sitting, motionless.

How still it is, he thought. Before going to bed,
Max turned on the outdoor lights, double-checked the
door locks and poked the window blinds open to peer
into the yard. He didn't see the green eyes, but he sure
could *feel* them.

His pillowcase drank sweat from his neck and
shoulders while sirens wailed far and near in all
directions: ambulances, police cruisers, fire trucks, car
alarms; each one a wreck, a fire, an auto break-in. He
lay awake thinking about green eyes and wondering if
the entire city had gone mad.

In the morning his coffee was as black and swirling
as his dreams had been. He could not remember them,
neither did he want to. All he knew was that something
monstrous kept coming for him. At least it was only in
his dreams, he realized. Max thought about the work in
front of him today and decided to drop by the library.

He'd been thinking about the Pacific Northwest lately, probably because so many of his friends had either been to or lived in Eugene, Seattle or Vancouver. He wanted to get some of those images in his head. What he got leaving the house, instead, was a face full of cobwebs. He saw the web -- attached to the door knob, overhead porch light and a branch from the hedge row -- at the last minute. But it was too late. He danced around, yelling, wiping off his face, hair and arms, wondering where the hell the spider was.

At the library, he found pictures of gnarled driftwood and misty cliffs -- images that would look great on walking sticks. Leaving, Max noted that one of the new books on display in the lobby featured medieval gargoyles. But the thing that stopped him dead in his tracks was the cover; on it was the leering face of the same gargoyle that had come out of his cane last night.

He forgot about the gargoyles, however, when he saw two e-mail orders waiting for him on his computer at home -- his first orders off the web. "Yeah," he shouted, pumping his fist in the air. "That's the way." Grabbing a beer, he went to the garage and opened the two windows. Bars of light slanted in, freeze-framing floating motes and dust particles in the air, and he reflected a moment while the fan began blowing. He loved the memories, dim as they were:

His grandfather's garage. There was an anvil; a workbench clamp flaking ancient red paint; an upright grinding stone as big as a tire, with an iron seat to sit in and foot pedals and straps to make it turn; the musty

Both customers, coincidentally, wanted snake designs. No problem. Max picked up a couple of mellow spruce sticks and knocked out the snakes in no time at all. *Money in the bank.*

Then he thought about the Northwest again. He looked over his sticks and selected an aspen: sharp lines and contours, nice whirl pattern, good texture. Just what he was looking for. Reminded him of Oregon, ocean, surf. Perched on his barstool, he looked at the 4-foot branch across his legs.

Take your time, he thought. *Do it right.* Surely last night's gargoyle had been a fluke, an aberration.

Max opened his cupboard shelf and pulled a White Rhino nug from a glass jar. He had a fat garden all last year in his basement, but he gave it up to make his cane business work. In the meantime, the guy he set up with his lights, fans and plants kept Max well-supplied with kind buds. He took a hit and exhaled the smoke over the stick, contemplating the carving lines like a surgeon studying placement of the first incision.

Then he placed the stick to his forehead and thought a few moments to see if it had anything to tell him. He saw birds, but they flew at him screeching, so real he felt compelled to duck. Max had to open his eyes to break the illusion, and he shook his head in disbelief.

"Get to work!" he barked to nothing and no one, nonetheless reassured to hear his voice boom in the room with authority. He turned on his fluorescent shop lights and began carving and sanding, chiseling and boring in earnest, losing himself completely in the wood, bringing out its beauty, creating on top of the cane a handle depicting a forest-and-cliff scene. Below, where the fingers grip the staff, he carved some ocean and a beach.

A few hours later he got a distinct feeling that someone was watching him. He wheeled around on his bar stool, half expecting to see a person staring at him from behind the old family Ford. But nada, nothing. However, the back of his neck was tingly, a feeling he'd never had before, and he suddenly felt completely tired; in fact, drained. He sat still, listening, for what he did not know. One minute he was fine; now he felt depression steal his good mood as he stared at spot on the stick where a mermaid's face could go -- just under the ocean waves; yeah, he would make a sweet face.

He got the hair right. It was all beautiful and spread, mixed in with the water, carved in an area about the size of a beer coaster. While working on the face, though, he became clammy and almost feverish. Still, he carved on. Somehow. Or, more to the point, although he held the instrument of shaping -- the chisel -- the design kept changing before his eyes. His hand was not his own, something else was guiding it -- had to be guiding it because the fair mermaid image on his walking stick was now a drowned face, crying out in terror.

There it was again: ugliness bubbling up from the darkest depths of Max's psyche. He cursed, flung the stick down in frustration and stormed from the shop.

Later his friend Dave came over with a 6-pack and they hung out for a couple hours playing video games and listening to CDs After Dave left, Max let his pit bull out, as usual. She bolted past the door and flew to the back yard like a heat-seeking missile, impacting an animal and rolling with it in a screeching ball of fangs and fur. Max grabbed a cane and ran over to see what he could do, but there was no need. Dozer had sunk her formidable jaws into a massive raccoon's neck and was shaking the life out of it, the body hitting the ground with dull thuds like a limp rag doll.

"Pull your dog off 'n' ah'll shoot the coon," Old Man Hockenmeister slurred at the fence, his thumb flicking the safety switch on a 12-gauge. He was weaving in a circle of sorts even though his feet were rooted to one place.

"Mr. Hockenmeister, please," Max said. "The coon's dead and I'll get my dog inside." Something about a drunk old man in a wife-beater T-shirt with a shotgun made Max nervous.

"I'm callin' SPC tomorrow," he slurred. "Have 'em check these critters for rabies."

"Yes, you do that," Max replied, trying to keep Dozer's nose out of the coon's guts. He knew the chances of Old Man Hockenmeister even remembering this event were slim. Wifeless for over a year, his descent into alcoholism had been rapid and dramatic.

Dozer, meanwhile, was panting like a sprinter and whipping her tail. Blood soaked her face, chest and front legs; and her lower lip was split. Further, a rake of four claw marks, each about three inches long, welled up on one side of her face. Max looked at the coon. He never knew they had such claws, long and black, like a miniature bear's.

At first he didn't understand why his dog had gone after the coon with such a vengeance, but when he was hosing Dozer off she caught him with her wise brown eyes and played the whole thing out for him, like a dream sequence, and he understood everything instantly:

The gargoyle had morphed into the raccoon and was coming for Max when Dozer slew it.

Max felt weird getting in bed, and it was hard to settle down. He thought he heard spiders scratching at his window, trying to get in. He sensed something out there: what, he did not know. But he felt it, just as sure as he felt the fear slowly fill him like water rising inside a stricken submarine. His thoughts drifted to a TV show he saw recently about Komodo dragons, how one chased down a little deer and broke its leg with a swipe of its powerful tail, then began eating the fawn while it cried. It was awful to watch or think about.

Max reached out and stroked Dozer's fat, pit bull head. "We'll get through it, buddy," he said, then added: "Thanks for killing the gargoyle tonight, Dozer. I love you."

In the morning he woke and showered. When he was washing his hair with his eyes closed his brain started processing visuals like he was standing in the middle of an interstate and all the traffic was careening

at him at 100 mph. Suddenly dizzy, he washed the soap
out of his hair and get his eyes open to stop spinning.

Then, when he was out of the shower and shaving,
an angry, red rash spread across his throat like a slit
from a scimitar. He felt sick to his stomach again, and
realized his hand began shaking.

Now Max realized he was officially desperate -- at
wit's end, and no matter what he did, he would have to
do it very carefully. After all, there were a million ways
to kill a guy, especially one who was haunted. Heck, he
was afraid to toast a piece of bread. And power tools?
Out of the question.

Of course he could try working again, but with the
way his luck was running his sticks would become
poisonous serpents or, he might accidentally burn the
garage down. Max could remember being this psyched
only twice before: once last year when he and his girl
split up and he was torn with grief for weeks; and the
other time when he got busted and was tripping so hard
he couldn't stop shaking.

In both instances, though, he at least knew hc
would survive. But now, with this bacteria oozing up
from his dark self, infecting his spirit, he began
doubting even that. He recalled stories of people
steering straight into oncoming traffic even though they
knew death was certain, yet being incapable of stopping
the impulse.

He realized that he would have to make a
conscious, deliberate decision to fight back, that he
could not keep drifting along hoping things would get
better. This thing was deeper than that. Through every
sense available to him -- his intuition, nervous system,

gut-feeling, ESP -- Max heard the armies of darkness closing in on him, blocking his exits with elaborate maneuvers. Through his telescope at night he saw the enemy warlords bent in their tents over candlelight and maps, planning his demise with meticulous precision.

He began making plans for the one place he felt safe, his own holy place, you could say: the Jemez Mountains in New Mexico, home to painted caves, cliff dwellings and an ancient volcano. He got out his maps and called his friend, Hector, who lived outside of Los Alamos. It was Hector who had showed him how and where to collect wood for carving; and Hector who showed Max The Place Where Spirits Walk, the ancient cliff dwellings.

Back in those days, Max and Anna were on their way to a Rainbow Gathering at Four Corners. They had spent a magical night in the Jemez Mountains, laughing, tripping mescaline, rolling down the sides of Bandera Volcano, naming the children they would never have and trying to count all the stars. Never in his life had Max seen so many stars; neither had he ever tripped so hard or been so much in love.

On the first day of his trip to New Mexico he figured he'd stop in the Oklahoma Panhandle for the night, but the setting sun and painted sky so awed Max with purple and orange colors that he found it easy to keep going. Earlier, when the sun was hottest and highest in the sky, the massive white clouds billowed and formed, in his eyes, Coronado and his Spanish columns, lances *en attencion*, trekking across the heavens on tired nags to loot civilizations, convert heathens and spread syphilis and smallpox.

Max enjoyed driving out West -- enjoyed the space of it all, the vastness. A person had room to think when he could see for miles around in all directions. And then there was the night, when a million stars began shining and the air was fresh and cool. He rolled up his window and smoked a joint. Midnight became 1 a.m. and 1 became 2; then, shortly afterwards Max saw blue lights flashing and rotating in the distance: *Flying saucer baby, that would be out of sight.* And why not? After all, he'd been seeing monsters lately. Space creatures didn't seem like that much of a stretch. And he was near Roswell.

Instead, a few miles later, a cow loomed up suddenly before him in the headlights. He wrenched the steering wheel so hard to the left to avoid hitting it that he almost rolled his Blazer. The road sloped into a valley and around a bend where state troopers and county sheriffs gathered around an overturned semi. Flames devoured the truck, licking the night sky and the driver hung stiffly from the cab window by his legs, a blackened scarecrow burning to a crisp.

Cows were strewn like broken toys, mooing and groaning pitifully, some crawling, bones punching through their hides. Then the troopers began shooting them and they cried even louder. Max watched them work, silhouetted against the flames, pistol arms jerking as each round blazed from their barrels, the revolvers sending sharp cracks echoing across the plains.

The acrid odor of gunpowder and sweet-sick smell of blood filled his lungs, and Max thought: *I'm standing at the gates of hell.* Shots kept hammering home, and after a while the cows made no noise at all. Dozer completely freaked out and began howling and barking and whining, doing 360-degree turns on the front seat. Max picked his way through the carnage as quickly as he could.

He told all this to Hector a few hours later while they ate some rice and beans. Hector got mad. "See?" he said. "That's cause you fuck with the cows in Nebraska. And their spirits are getting back at the people who killed them. Did you see where that truck was from? Probably Nebraska, man; probably your hometown -- Omaha."

Hector hated packing plants for two reasons: he thought killing animals was morally wrong, and he detested the beef industry for hiring his Indian and Latino brothers to do the shit jobs in slaughter houses.

Hector hustled Mike off to bed, reminding him that he would need his rest. When he and Max talked on the phone last week, Hector had pointed out that tonight the moon would be full -- a good time for Max to dive inside himself and confront the demons vying for his mind. Hector was an astrologer, among many other things. Of course he had volunteered to go to the mountain with his gringo friend. The foot of the volcano -- one of their favorite places -- was where they'd met, both gathering sticks at the time. Hector was the first master carver Max had known, and taught him much about wood.

Max woke and found Hector on the porch beginning a cane, the long strips of aspen falling from the branch as he straightened it with his knife. He paused occasionally to hold the staff up and sight down it like a gunsmith.

"'Sup, brother," Max said, groggily rubbing the sleep from his eyes with the heels of his hands.

Hector smiled. "Can't stay away from the magic mountain, huh? Better move down here, bro."

Max laughed. "It is something to think about, that's for sure." And a little voice inside him added: *No, really. Why don't you move out of that frickin city you live in? Everyone else does.*

He watched the shavings, long and curly like Hector's hair, pile up on the porch. Soon the skin was off the stick and a straight, white staff was emerging.

"And the cocoon becomes a butterfly," Max said.

"Si senor," Hector replied, adding: "Hungry? We should eat and get it digested because we'll damn sure be throwing up when we eat the peyote."

They chased their vitamins down after supper with ginkgo and ginseng tea and retired to the living room, where they pulled some tubes and watched the news and weather. Clear skies and a full moon, just what the doctor ordered.

The drive to the campsite was only 10 minutes away. Hector bounced down a dirt road and pulled off to park behind a clump of trees, where they loaded up their gear and walked down to the river with the dogs. Hector took off his shoes and tied them around his neck by the strings, then put Cujo across his neck like a lamb. Max did the same with Dozer. "Follow me," Hector instructed, wading across the knee-deep, swift-flowing water to a sandbar, where he came up and stuck his cane in the ground. "Here," he said. "Good place to camp."

Setting up was easy since Hector had already been to the island and collected firewood. Soon a kettle whistled and the dogs had explored the sandbar and settled down by the fire. They would stay behind tonight and guard the sleeping bags and food supplies.

Hector pulled the peyote buttons from his backpack and Max helped pound them between two rocks. The pulverized peyote was then scraped into their mugs of steaming tea, and they sat -- backs against their packs -- sipping the tripping brew, burning bowls of ganja, waiting for the peyote visions to begin.

After a while, Hector lit a big shock of sage and began playing a flute. Its sound was both sad and haunting, joyful and proud, spiritual and contemplative. A wind gust raced by and carried the notes off to the mighty mountain, where they soared up its steep flanks and plunged into its caldera as if the huge volcano harbored a black hole eating everything, even music.

Max was getting good and lost in that thought when Hector interrupted: "Look at the moon, brother," he said. Ripe, fat, swollen, it rose fast as a helium balloon, a huge ivory disc flecked with silver. Hector lay his flute down upon the Hopi-woven blanket. A shooting star arced across the heavens, and the yin energy of night gathered her shawl around New Mexico. Hector began chanting in the sound of the Indian. Max closed his eyes and drifted, saw in his mind the image of a hawk, and he became the raptor, or at least its companion soaring high over the sun-splashed mesas, plunging into the golden canyons.

"Hey--Ohhh--Hey--Ohhh" Hector chanted, his voice strong and earnest, painful and mournful, flowing down the streams and into the rivers of time and space in the land of his ancestors.

Suddenly Max was spinning in a centrifuge, sweat pouring from his body. He rolled away from the fire just in time. His stomach tossed out the peyote, and when it was done his head was in the sand and he was alone. Max brushed his face off. The spinning had stopped, and he was feeling mental instead of physical, a nice change indeed. In fact, his head was as clear as the mountain air.

A white-hot ember popped between the logs, disappearing in a poof of consummation. *Ashes to ashes*, Max thought, feeling so completely insignificant, a speck of nothing in the universe. He gazed up at the infinity of space in the night sky and became frustrated at his own smallness and irrelevance in the grand scheme of things. *He wanted to make a difference in the world, but how? Where?*

Coyotes serenading the moon brought him back to the physical world. Max drank draughts of the rich air -- spruce, pine, and aspen-scented, his lungs a bellows, filling, expanding, intoxicating. Then he heard the flying things, crawling things and swimming things. He heard them all: the wing flap, tail slap, frog croak, cricket chirp, snake slither. The armadillo scuttle. And a kinship with nature stirred in his soul; instead of feeling like a speck of nothing he felt linked to a thriving, teeming ecosystem -- a partner with earth and its pulse. Their heartbeats and his heartbeats and respect for all living things merged together and surrounded him in a whirling vortex, and he left the physical world once again and surfed the spiritual plane for a while where he saw things of such wonder he could never describe them.

He was meditating when he heard flute music again. Max opened his eyes and rose slowly, looking around. Atop a cliff bank downstream he saw Hector, blue-white electricity sizzling off his fingers as he played, rocking back and forth, up and down, dancing a jig like old Kokopelli himself. Max laughed with glee, cupped his hands to his mouth and shouted: "Hello Kokopelli, what mischief are you creating tonight?" and he ran to catch him, but by the time he'd climbed to the spot, Hector was gone.

So Max headed for The Place Where Spirits Walk, the base of the mountain. There, from sockets carved in sheer volcanic cliff, 13th Century Indian caves gazed down upon a rocky plateau. It would be impossible to tell how many weddings, harvest celebrations and religious ceremonies had been held at the base of the volcano over the centuries. And it was true that the vast majority of those ancient players had evolved -- gone on to other systems and new karma. But a few remained, fighting the old feuds, trying to bury hatchets in each other's backs, keeping the old vendettas alive.

Such it was tonight: A scorpio full moon shone on two warriors trying to settle an old score. Max came upon the clearing and saw two kachinas clashing with spears -- one clad in wolf skin, the other in white buffalo -- stabbing to a rhythm Max knew as Hector's flute music. Their sweat was silver liquid under the moonlight, muscles dark and shaded, neck veins throbbing, sparring staffs sending violent whacks and clacks across the enchanted landscape.

White Buffalo kachina tried hooking Wolf kachina, but Wolf slashed back, raking Buffalo with his fangs. Max paused, momentarily mesmerized by the fighting Indian spirits. He wasn't sure if the kachinas were real or not, but he didn't want to risk drawing their attention by moving, so he froze and stared, the peyote ringing his head like three-alarm fire bells.

The warriors swirled before him -- horns, howls and teeth -- until finally, Wolf went down with a cry. While White Buffalo danced his victory celebration Max skirted the clearing and moved up the volcano's flanks, chugging and huffing toward the top.

When he was about half-way up the volcano it seemed to gurgle and rumble itself awake, and he felt rivers of lava roaring through the mountain's underground caverns, blasting its vent shafts, tumbling back down its inner hills and valleys, shooting up again, warming the stone beneath his feet. *This damn thing's alive,* he thought, listening to the thunder-booms below.

And why the hell was he going up the peak, he wondered? He wasn't real clear on that one himself, but he did know that something was drawing him to the summit as surely as flight draws arrows. Was it the impulse to crest the heights and stand triumphant -- the great stag -- defiant to the end, staring death in the eyes and giving it the finger? Or perhaps death wasn't waiting for him at the top after all; maybe some good stuff was up there. *That's it. Hector's up there waiting. We'll share a thermos of hot ginseng tea and smoke some hooters, get righteous.*

Then Max had to concentrate on climbing because his breath was getting ragged. He trekked for another hour before he reached the summit, and when he did the view was so awesome he took deep breaths, trying to fill his lungs with the holy spirit -- any kind of holy spirit. On the volcano's rim -- one of the highest points in the southwest -- the moon was as big as a dinner plate, so close Max could have pulled it down and eaten supper off it. Stars twinkled so near he could have plucked them, too. For miles in all directions, canyons and counties radiated the moon's silvery light. But something else was tugging at the coat sleeve of his mind, a vibe from inside the crater, it seemed; so, although the back of his neck was tingling ominously, Max dropped to all fours and crawled to the edge, peering over cautiously.

The far side, half a mile across, was shrouded in shifting, swirling mist, and as he got closer to the edge that old fearful sick feeling spread in his stomach like gangrene. Then, chin over the rim, looking downward to the center of the crater, the caldera -- the 1,000-foot drop to the lava pits -- a strong gust of wind came up at his back, almost pushing him over; and simultaneously, a bat swooped down on Max from behind, actually beating his head with a flap of its wing, almost forcing him over the edge for the long drop. At the last minute he quickly grabbed a scraggly bush to avoid being swallowed by the mountain.

And he stared into the vast pit, the black void, feelings of hopelessness smothering his soul, eclipsing his spirit. He was so fed up with this corrupt world! And so close to oblivion. Do it! Do it! Do it! a chorus of voices insisted, and it dawned on Max like the proverbial ton of bricks that he could very well add his bones to the bottom of the volcano along with all its other victims over the centuries -- the accidents, suicides, virgin sacrifices, lovers' leapers and traitors cast in the crater, not to mention the murdered. Yes, he could add his bones to that lot right now, leaning forward, almost over the edge.

But there was another voice, too, in direct opposition to the caldera's siren call. This voice was soft and gentle and calling Max's name. He turned and saw a woman coming . . . seemingly floating up the trail rather than walking it. How that could be he didn't know. But she was coming all right, and not even breaking a sweat. Max stared at her, his heart pounding, head spinning, not trusting his eyes.

Frickin peyote's wiggin me out.

Not that he was complaining. Staring at the Indian maiden walking up the mountain was better than talking to the volcano, he reckoned. As she came up the path Max could have sworn a halo, or at least *some* type of light, glowed around her. *Jeez,* he thought, *put her in the movies . . . princess to the bold chief who leads the warriors.* She walked up like she'd known him all her life.

"Hello," she said. "What's going on in the crater tonight?"

Max was speechless. "Uh, uh; uh-hu," he stammered. "I'm fine . . . and the crater; well, weird stuff. I was getting spooked." Although he was struck dumb for the most part his eyes and brain took in the facts: the woman in moccasins before him was about 25 years old, wore a long deer skin skirt and shirt with a peach-colored shawl around her shoulders. Simple turquoise-and-silver earrings and a turquoise necklace were her only jewelry. Her throat was soft and brown, and her high cheekbones made her look mysterious and proud.

"Care if I join you?"

Are you kidding?

Please, sit down beside me.

Max shook his head no, still convinced this woman before him was a peyote vision or that somehow Hector was playing a prank on him. Max turned around and looked for him. "Very funny you bastard!" he shouted, certain that Hector lurked nearby. "I'll get you for this!"

"Hector's fine," the mirage said. "I saw him earlier at the base. But let's talk about you. You've been through so much with your demon-fights. But you must know you're going to be okay."

"Thank you, but who are you?" Max finally sputtered. "How did you get here?"

"My name is Quannah. And I got here the same way you did -- by hiking up the mountain. You don't see any wings on my back, do you?" she asked, rotating her torso and dipping her shoulders toward Max.

She had him there. "Where did you come from?" he asked. "Are you from around here?"

"Yes," she said, running her fingers through her long hair and sweeping it over her shoulder.

Like a crow's wing, Max thought.

She smiled: "I've always been from around here."

"What do you mean by that?" Max said.

"I mean, everybody's from someplace and I'm from here. I really haven't traveled anywhere else."

Her English was perfect, which, for some reason, surprised him. Still, he wasn't convinced she was real, so he was a little abrupt. She stared back at him, completely neutral. "Look," she said, "You're going to have to be a little nicer than that. I didn't hike all the way up this mountain to be interrogated."

Max blushed. "I sorry. No offense. I'm tripping peyote right now and things are crazy." He kicked a rock in front of him, then looked at Quannah and grinned: "I guess you're real."

"Of course I am," she laughed, poking him in the ribs. "I mean, we're having this conversation, aren't we?"

She had him there. "Okay," he said. "You got me. It still seems weird, though, you and me chatting away like old friends on top of the mountain."

She shrugged. "Do you know how many conversations have gone down up here over the ages? If you counted them all, it'd be a lot. No," she continued, "Old Mother here has heard a lot of talking over the years," and she patted the mountain affectionately. "By the way," she said. "You sure ask a lot of questions."

"I'm sorry. I've been going crazy lately. Things haven't been fun."

"Go on," she said. "I'm listening."

"Wait," Max said, "Why did you say I'd been through so much when you saw me . . . like you've been watching me or something. What's up with that?"

"I saw it on your face, silly."

He thought about that for a minute, then went on: "Well, a few minutes ago I just about threw myself in the volcano for some reason. Or something tried to throw me in. I'm not quite sure which. And lately I've had so much stuff seething around inside me: ugly, violent stuff. Tonight it's coming out man, all the ghosts and goblins. I'm either gonna explode or get some shit resolved, one way or another."

Then he was telling her about his cane business and the carving nightmare it had become -- the ugly feeling of being haunted -- when a shooting star streaked across the sky, followed by another. "Whoaaa," he said. "Did you see that?"

She nodded. "You see, there's beauty along with ugliness." She smiled at him with understanding and put her hand on his arm reassuringly. Her touch was light but extraordinary. It filled him almost immediately with peace and a type of contentment, and the heaviness he'd been carrying on his shoulders like Atlas suddenly evaporated. He looked up, and at least a dozen shooting stars criss-crossed heaven, racing through the sky.

Quannah stood and held her shawl over her head, spinning around and making happy laughing sounds, catching the wind. Max watched her dance in front of the moon.

Which reminded him: "Hey," he hollered, "the moon's supposed to be in Scorpio tonight. Hector said I'd be in for a treat."

"That's one way to put it," Quannah replied. "Do you know what house your moon falls in your birth chart?"

He did know. "Hector said the twelfth house, whatever that means."

"Well, that does make things interesting," Quannah said. "Let's see. We're talking about your illusions, your subconscious, confinements both real and imagined. These are the themes you've been working through. Some heavy stuff."

She explained how she had grown up with astrology and a mix of tribal shamanism and earth-based worship. "In fact," she concluded, "the ancient arts have always been practiced here. It's what makes this place so interesting. Of course, once they weren't ancient; in Atlantean days, they were pretty contemporary. My people, in fact, used to trade with the Atlanteans: grain for fruit, rice for ganja; and of course, both nations exchanged ambassadors and formed alliances against common foes. We also had help from the extra-terrestrials."

"What happened? Where did it all go?"

"Cortez rode through in 1535. Things haven't been the same since."

"Wow," Max said. A part of him was fading. He felt tired all of a sudden.

Quannah reached out and put her hand on his forehead. And this time her touch was not only cool, but calming again, which was good because Max felt something like a panic attack coming on. But Quannah shut the door on whatever was trying to rear up from the darkest depths of his worst nightmares.

Yet he was still cold. Max buttoned his flannel shirt and hugged himself for warmth and, seeing it, Quannah soundlessly moved beside him and put her shawl over his shoulders. Then he was swimming around in a peyote pond like a lazy fish, and she was singing, chanting hypnotically, louder and louder, and began telling a story:

"A tribe lived in peace at the foot of this mountain. One day Blue Coats came on their horses and slaughtered every living thing. Blood of women and children turned the snow red. Brains and guts steamed in the cold air. Maidens raped and murdered and thrown in the river, the dead flowers of the tribe, floating away with red pouring from their bodies. And the Earth cried.

"The last batch of wood you got here was from that village spot. You had no way of knowing, but you should never have taken those limbs and branches. Their roots drank the blood and pain of the lost Jemez tribe. Like those poor people, that wood was cursed -- filled with the White Man's hatred and the Red Man's grief. But you have fought well. You're going to be okay. Just make sure you burn the old cursed wood when you get home."

Max rested at Hector's most of the next day and hit the road toward evening, driving at night when the air was cool. Again the moon shone so brightly he could have driven without headlights

He saw the rich assortment of wood -- about 20 fine looking staffs -- in back of his truck when he stopped for gas in Kansas. Max had no idea how the sticks got there. Hector? Quannah? Whomever it was, they had kicked him down some of the most beautiful wood he'd ever seen: swirled, rich, dense. He would carve some beautiful canes from it, just as soon as he got home and burned the sticks in his garage.

He lit a joint and rolled down his window, whistling to the honky-tonk radio station and driving to freedom.

Jail Bait

You could say Tom cared just a little too much for his prison students.

Tom's boss was an academic meteor with a pretty blonde head on her shoulders and a fine mind spinning around in it like a centrifuge. She made all the right moves at all the right times and was headed straight for the top because her male bosses thought she was terrific. Wrapped thus in their cloak of patriarchal protection, Assistant Dean Ann Anderson interacted with subordinates with a sense of invincibility and arrogance, although she tried to hide those vices by pretending to be nice.

Only she wasn't.

Tom had dealt with her for a couple years now. So when she suggested he teach at the state prison out on the river he was speechless. He knew that cute smile she flashed and the Sioux City Kid grin she wore masked the fact that she would stick a knife in him or anyone else blocking her way as she leap-frogged over the dead bodies on her way to the top.

So was this Machiavellian charmer offering him a gift or a curse?

Prison! A word as bad to Tom as the word *cancer*, a word he always shoved out of his mind when it got there because people like him went to prison all the time, even though he served ten years in the military, earned a master's degree, owned a home, paid taxes, raised a family and taught college English classes.

Why did people like Tom go to prison all the time? Because Tom not only smoked weed, he also grew it. So did all of his friends. Did it matter to them that they lived in a Red State run by Republicans who liked throwing marijuana smokers in jail? Oh hell no. Buckle down to these people, follow their lousy laws and you lose your soul, he figured. So Tom and his friends considered themselves part of the resistance. He had fought for people's freedom in Iraq; he figured he could do the same here.

He refocused his attention on Assistant Dean Anderson. Responsible for juggling the appointments of hundreds of Metro Community College part-time instructors each academic quarter, she held incredible power over adjuncts like Tom who viewed one of her full-time teaching jobs as a dream come true. Those beauties came with fifty-thousand dollars a year and a host of benefits. Sadly, those jobs went to a mere quarter of the community college faculty. The remaining seventy-five percent of instructors were part-timers like Tom who limped along on peanuts and the hope that one day they'd be promoted to full-time.

"Honestly," he said. "Teaching in prison never crossed my mind."

Oh the irony. Tom was growing marijuana and his boss wanted him to go into prison and teach people who were in jail for growing marijuana!

"I know you're a good teacher," she said. "That's why I'm asking you first. With your military background, you're the best person I have to teach those prisoners. This hasn't been done before. It's a new pilot program."

What she wasn't telling Tom was that she'd already offered the job to scores of instructors, part-time and full, and they'd all turned her down.

Damn that woman! He had to be careful with her. She already had him driving all over the county three days a week this academic quarter: a morning class out west with spoiled suburban kids; a night class up north at the "ghetto branch" of the junior college. Then there was the southwestern campus and the downtown campus. He'd taught at all of them the past decade. Now prison?

"So we're talking about me – "

" – teaching a beginning composition class the first academic quarter, then moving that class to the next quarter with writing research papers. And with any luck, the word on your fantastic teaching has spread and students are signing up for another English I composition class and then you're teaching two classes in jail."

He didn't know whether to say *Lucky Me* or not. True, she could have offered the jail gig to someone else.

Yet he paused.

Then she dangled the carrot in front of him. "You know," she said, stretching out the word k-n-o-w and leaning forward with a whispering confidence in a conspiratorial air like a rebel fomenting a palace coup to depose a monarch, "there's a full-time position opening up next year." And with that she opened the fingers of both hands resting in front of her on her desk, as if releasing miniature and celebratory balloons of revelation into the air, illuminating his path to success if he would only go forth and do her bidding as a prison teacher.

She'd lured him into teaching traps before with promises and bribes, then forgotten about him once he accepted her assignment. Consequently, more than once Tom had found himself driving home on ice rinks in winter after teaching a night class on the far side of town. And there were plenty of other times he started classes at eight in the morning just so full-timers wouldn't have to; no, early morning and late night classes were for adjuncts like Tom. And apparently prison classes were, too.

So there he was his first morning sitting in his car in the penitentiary parking lot staring at the foreboding prison, a sprawling one-story series of red brick buildings surrounded by a chain link fence topped with razor wire and a guard tower.

Jesus, he said to himself. What have I gotten myself into?

He reached into his back pocket and fished out something he carried with him to remind himself why he taught, particularly on days like this; then whispered along with the words as he read Saint Francis's prayer: *Lord, make me an instrument of your peace;*

where there is hatred, let me sow love; where there is injury, pardon;

where there is doubt, faith; where there is despair, hope;

where there is darkness, light; and where there is sadness, joy.

Then he got out of his car, walked across the lot and went inside the prison. Getting processed was like going through an airport security line. Tom put his teaching bag on the conveyor belt, the machine ate it and an imposing athletic black guard in his fifties at the other end said You must be the new college guy. Tom said Yes sir and was waved through the security arch that would sound an alarm if he were carrying a weapon.

Tom's bag exited the x-ray machine and the black guard said he wouldn't search him like a regular visitor. The guard also wished Tom luck, adding: "Be careful in there. Don't trust those prisoners for anything. They in here for a reason."

"Gotcha," Tom said.

Those words kept turning in his head as he walked across the courtyard. *Don't trust those prisoners for anything.* He thought that sounded rough. Wasn't everyone here to help rehabilitate the prisoners? And how could you do that if they didn't think you trusted them?

He met with the educational coordinator of the prison, a pinched and nervous woman just hitting menopause who wore what appeared to be a home-knit wool vest and a long skirt down to her booted feet. Her hair was short and going black to grey, and Tom found himself looking at the top of her head, which was balding, as she explained prison protocols to him. Her eyes were fish eyes: big, round and bulging from her pale and colorless face.

Tom saw that she walked with a slight limp as he followed her down a long hallway empty as a ghost town and with floors waxed and buffed to a sheen. She stopped in front of a door, mumbled "Good luck" and shuffled back down the hallway, looking to him for all the world like an orderly in an insane asylum.

Tom now felt like he would be hacked to pieces upon entering the room by a bunch of alpha males. The thought made him laugh. He was not a typical academic geek who would rather write about what experience is rather than go out and have one. He had been an active-duty soldier and had two Iraq tours under his belt. Tom didn't have much ego. He never browbeat students or made them feel bad because he started off at the bottom as a soldier and knew all about authority and saluting and being low man on the totem pole.

He threw open the door and strode into the room, saw the assembled class of twenty or so men sitting in chairs and plopped his satchel with a thud on a table in front of them. "What's up? This is a weird damn place, know it?" he said in agitation.

Silence. Complete, absolute, utter silence.

Who in the hell was this guy and how did he get in here talking like this?

Of course they didn't know what to expect.

He bonded with his students quickly because they were edgy bastards like he was. They saw it in him and he saw it in them. And actually, teaching prisoners was no more difficult for Tom than teaching normal students was. He was a natural teacher who truly focused on motivating students to express themselves with words. He helped each one on his paper, gave them the tools to build paragraphs, pointed them in the right direction, then let them do the work. In a way it was simple. "Meet me halfway," he told his students, "and I'll be there with a helping hand for you."

The subject of marijuana came up rather quickly. After all, some of the poor fellows were in the pokey for smoking it in one way or another. Damn straight they wanted to write about it. Now that would be a class they could brag about in the chow hall later on. *Professor letting me write a paper on marijuana! Fucking A.*

The subject rose one day in class while discussing potential topics for their first paper: a ten-page argumentative essay compete with thesis, main points, supporting details and a proper beginning, middle and end. A prisoner named Jim who couldn't have been more than twenty asked if he could write a paper on marijuana.

"Of course you can," Tom replied. "That's probably what got you here in the first place," and the whole class cracked up. Then he got serious and told them they could write about anything they wanted to because this was college and they were here to explore the world of ideas by writing about some of them.

One month turned into another and Tom was gratified to see the majority of students trying their best as they wrote academic essays incorporating the principles of composition such as cause and effect; compare and contrast; explaining and evaluating; and speculating about causes. The majority made As and Bs because he taught them well and they knew they could get a good grade in his class if they worked hard, which they did.

Prison teaching wasn't all fun and games. Sometimes it was challenging for Tom to remember that he had to see the men as people, not felons and bad guys, or he wouldn't be able to teach them. That was sometimes difficult. One prisoner in particular made him sick to his stomach. A school bus driver who one day arranged his route so a little girl on his bus would be last dropped off. But he didn't drop her off. He drove somewhere and molested her. Tom remembered reading that story in the paper.

And then one day that monster bus driver was in front of Tom as a student and it was Tom's job to teach him and this kid was sweaty-pudgy with pale skin and looked like a namby-pamby boy, not the type at all Tom was used to in the Army, and he just wanted to punch the pervert in the face for being a child molester. But then he had to gut-check himself and remind himself why he was here.

. . . where there is hatred, let me sow love;
where there is injury, pardon.

Besides, those child molesters got their own. One day he was in class and a group in the corner were smiling and smacking their fists against the open palm of their other hand and Tom said: What's up?

They laughed and one of them explained that a bus full of child molesters – CHIMOS in prison slang – was coming in from the state pen in Lincoln.

So the CHIMOS didn't need Tom giving them attitude. Apparently they got the shit beat out of themselves by other prisoners. "Remember," an older prisoner once said to Tom as they worked his paper: "I'm a father of daughters, and so are many others here. What do you think we do to child molesters when we see them?"

Yes, there was a certain brutality to prison that Tom sidestepped with his students so he could focus on providing them a clean, bright place of learning and acceptance, for he knew you can't have one without the other. Was Tom the only person who didn't judge them? He somehow felt a need to be that person.

Tom had gotten all hollowed out back there in Iraq and done some bad things that he needed forgiven for. He figured being non-judgmental in the prisoners' lives and sincerely trying to help them might make him a redeemable human being.

And so he taught.

Who were the prisoners? As Tom found out, they were a lot of people. Some were drunk drivers who messed up really bad, like the welder from Alaska who drove a car with one too many and took out a father and son driving home from a college hockey game. Tom would never forget the look on the poor guy's face when he said he had absolutely no memory of it. "I woke up in the hospital," he said. "I was handcuffed to the bed rail. I asked why and they said 'Do you know what you just did?' and I said No, what? Then they told me."

Others were like Hank, a friendly guy around thirty with red hair and a trim beard who farmed out west by North Platte. Hank looked like any number of graduate students Tom had gone to school with, but he had a different story. His marriage didn't work out and his wife took to running around in a small town where everyone knew about it and, after the divorce, somehow she got custody of the baby. Hank, despondent, quit his day job in town, took to drinking, got a DUI, fell behind on child-support payments and landed in prison.

"Now how am I going to make child-support payments if I'm in jail and can't earn no money?" he asked.

Tom had to admit Hank had a point.

Plenty of the prisoners had been drug-busted. But the guys in jail for dealing powder and pills – meth, coke, opiates – weren't really around. Tom's students were the pot smokers. Like Jose who ran kilos in south Omaha, or LaRon who flipped quarter pounds in the hood, and Mick who grew six plants until forty officers smashed down his door, shot his dog and hauled him off to jail. Mick was so bitter over all of it. His beloved pit bull shot over six plants.

One portion of the prisoner population Tom never saw was the crazy people, and inmates rarely spoke of them. Indeed, just as legions of underpaid part-time instructors were academia's dirty little secret, no one ever spoke of the number of locked-up insane in America's prisons. Slow-witted, unknowing and easily fooled, crazy people drifted through the penal system like shrimp, everyone's favorite meal.

Guards tricked them into discipline infractions constantly. A punch here, a kick there followed by the inevitable freak-out that brought on the straight-jacket crew and the take-down that led to ten days in the hole and cleaning fluid mixed in with the drinks they slid through the feeding slot. Guards did this for fun, Tom was told. Sure, his students said, a few of the guards were decent human beings. But most were uneducated gun-loving racists with mean streaks.

Then there was the black crew. God bless the black crew! Why they took to Tom he'd never know, but one of them saved his ass once and Tom was forever grateful. On that particular day, Tom was handing out the first graded essays. They had all been working on them together for three weeks and rewriting them and talking about them and today was the day it was all over. Many of the students earned As and Bs; then there was a bottom quarter of the class that got Cs. There were no Ds or Fs. The prisoner-students knew they could attend this class and do the work or they could sit in their cells and rot.

However, a big white kid named Nick doing a ten-year stretch for armed robbery sat in the back row and goofed off a lot. Tom handed out papers to the students around Nick. They were all As and Bs. Nick was busy rubber-necking, checking out the grades of his classmates. Then he got his paper -- a big fat C.

Back in front of the class, Tom saw that Nick had become an enraged bull and that he, Tom, must be the matador. And here Nick came, head down and angry. He got halfway up the aisle, just abreast of Marcus, one of the older blacks serving a life sentence for murder, and Marcus said: "Sitch yo ass down boy."

Nick froze dead in his tracks beside Marcus. Stood there glowering at Tom and then looking at Marcus. Once Tom was working with Marcus on an ending for his paper and Marcus told him how he smoked marijuana with embalming fluid on it. Why would you do that? Tom asked. Marcus said that stuff got you high as shit – too high.

"I murdered three people on it," he said. "I fucked up bad, drew me a life sentence."

No one challenged Marcus. He was smart, dapper too. Thin mustache, always clean-shaven. A neat and tidy man all the way down to his fingernails. Tom supposed Marcus survived by deciding to best the fools around him in their own game. He could lift a finger and have a man killed. So in class that day with Nick glowering at Tom and wanting to fight him . . . that was a moment, to be sure. Every man held his breath when Marcus told Nick to sit down.

And Nick did. He went back to his desk. Just like that.

So what happened in class wasn't all fun and games and walks through parks with pals and chums. This was prison. And king of all the emotions was frustration: frustration at getting caught; frustration at the judge who sentenced them; the ex-wife who chiseled them; the prison guards who mistreated them; the "friend" who testified against them; the judge who turned down their appeal. All of it was frustrating, from the minute inmates woke up in the morning until the minute they went to sleep at night. In many ways the prisoners had nothing in common, but when it came to frustration, resignation and anger, all were fellow travelers on that same voyage.

Tom tried keeping his talks with students centered on building the standard array of English essays; after all, he was a teacher. Yet sometimes the personal slipped in, not just for the students but for him, too. Once he stood in the yard on a beautiful spring day saying goodbye to Hank and a silver airliner from the nearby airport climbed skyward, sunlight glinting off its silver wings.

"Wouldn't you like to be on it?" Hank asked.

Tom nodded. "Yeah I would. Headed to Jamaica."

"With a cold drink on the tray in front of you." Hank said, then added: "You ever been to the islands?"

Tom snorted. "Man, I been broke my entire life. Only vacation I ever took was to Iraq courtesy of Uncle Sam, which was a bummer because he wanted me to kill people."

Hank registered surprise. "I thought you guys teaching college made big bucks."

"The professors and the deans make all the money," Tom said. "The rest of us part-timers trying to scratch out a living are just slaves on their academic plantation.

"I had no idea," Hank replied with a semi-stunned look.

"Me neither," Tom said. "When I was an enlisted swine in the Army I thought a master's degree would really be something special. So I went out and got one and now I'm broke as a joke. You can't get out of prison and I'm too broke to get out of Omaha. Not much difference, is there?"

The personal also slipped in at times like when Tom was working with Johnny Walking Stick, a half-Mexican, half-Native American coke dealer in south Omaha before a federal task force took him down. Johnny was a jailhouse lawyer who spent most of his

181

time in the prison library filing appeals and acting as his own attorney.

Today, Tom and Johnny were working on a cause and effect essay on alcoholism when Johnny said: "That goddamn bar!" referring to the inn just upriver from the prison.

"What's wrong with the Ship Ahoy Inn?" Tom asked.

Summertime, Johnny explained, bands played outdoors and the wind blew the music and laughter down into the prison yard where they could all hear it. "You want to be out there so bad," he said. "But you fucked up and that's why you're here. It's rough, man."

"Loss of freedom is a tough thing," Tom said. "There's no way around it."

Johnny could have also told Tom about the midnight train that rolled along the tracks down by the river five nights a week, how its lonesome whistle made a man feel as he lay on his bunk in a cage buried under mountains of regret, thinking about what could have been but wasn't. Thinking of sweethearts and loved ones.

Spring rolled around. Most of the students in Tom's class signed up for his Composition II class and he was delighting them with the joys of writing academic research papers. He was also shepherding another flock of Composition I inmate-students who signed on once they heard that Tom was good-natured and treated a man with dignity.

Tom sat in front of Ann's desk. She had Tom's student evaluations from the class he'd just taught. "So how's it going in jail?" she asked.

"Holding my own," he replied with a smile.

"These evaluations are very good," she said. "Would you like to see them?"

Of course he would.

She pushed the folder across her desk, making him get out of his chair to fetch it.

Best teacher ever. Really knows how to get me interested in English. Love this class.

All were variations on this theme. And yet . . .

Tom could feel something in her.

"Yes?" he asked.

"Maybe too good," she said.

He cocked a quizzical eyebrow.

She continued. "You were in the military, right."

"Yes Ma'am," he replied in mock-earnest.

"Well maybe you could be more – how can I say it? -- *military* with them. And remember: don't trust them for anything. They're crooks and con artists, muggers and thieves.

"Well dang my friendly hide!" he exclaimed with a cowboy drawl.

She looked at him, cocked a wry grin on one side of her mouth and said nothing.

Tom read the tea leaves and said Okay, he would give military a try.

One afternoon he was working on an informative essay with Jim and the subject of getting anything you wanted in prison came up. It was a loosey-goosey culture, Jim explained, where the guards and staff sort of looked "the other way" at contraband. Sure, they'd have no-knock surprise checks a few times a year, and people would get busted. But that was about it.

"People even smuggle marijuana in here," Jim said. "Plenty of it."

"You get some?" Tom asked.

Jim explained that the Mexicans kept it for themselves and so did the blacks. The white boys just had powder, which Jim disdained.

So Tom began smuggling weed into prison out of sorrow for Tom and his friends in jail for growing it or selling it. As far as Tom was concerned he saw nothing wrong with commercing in marijuana -- nature's medicine. And he knew how he'd feel if he was locked up and couldn't cop a buzz. He'd be effing going crazy with depression. So he smuggled in just enough to get them high. Jim had told Tom how easy it was to stuff a few grams of finely ground marijuana into an empty pen, and that's how Tom got it in. They might search his bag. But him?

Sure, the game was Russian roulette. Would Tom get stopped at the entry gate one day and really get searched – taken to the side room for the once-over until they found his marijuana stash inbound for the prisoners? He'd certainly seen others pulled aside and randomly searched: visiting friends, parents or girlfriends.

He knew it was crazy, but getting searched was the chance he was willing to take. Deep down inside, he was a marijuana outlaw thumbing his nose at The Man and his police state full of jails filled with marijuana smokers. Tom had fought for peoples' freedom in Iraq. And as far as he was concerned, he was fighting for these prisoners' 420 freedom by bringing some in for them.

Of course, that's not the way Assistant Warden Bobby Jo Overholzer would have seen it. She was a real toe-the-line kind of girl who never saw a rule that she didn't want to follow. Short, stout, a human fire hydrant with a mop of frizzy-red hair, she had an odd habit of staring at people accusingly like an angry priest searching a parishioner's soul for guilt, a woman who had bent many a man to the cross of repentance. Since her initials were B.J., the prisoners of course referred to her as "Blowjob" Overholzer.

Her second-in-command, Lieutenant Tammy Betcher, was her physical opposite -- a tall, gangly woman with a prominent jaw and large, dingy teeth. High school junior ROTC, community college associate's degree in criminal justice, top of her class for correctional custody guards. A real go-getter.

A charter member of the Geek Squad and a fun gal to go out with. She fancied herself a keen-eyed hawk who swooped in without warning upon the prisoners – the scared little mice – and took their treasure from them, be it alcohol, drugs or shivs.

In truth, though she always strove for snap and precision, she invariably ended up with a crooked gig line, a uniform blouse that needed ironing, plus an irritating habit of being a few minutes late for virtually *everything*.

The rolling joke old prisoners played on new ones went like this: "Will Assistant Warden B.J. Overholzer give you a blow job if you ask her nice?"

And the correct answer was always: "You Betcher!"

Tom kept playing marijuana roulette, though infrequently; so if he taught four times, he'd bring weed in once: a few grams stuffed inside a pen.

Then one Tuesday morning Assistant Warden Overholzer strode into his class unannounced with Lieutenant Betcher in tow "to look at the carpet," she said. They stared at it for a minute, then turned and watched him. He paused and looked at them with raised eyebrows . . .

"Go ahead," Assistant Warden Overholzer urged. "Don't mind us -- keep teaching." Then she and Lieutenant Betcher stared at him again for a few minutes, as if they were trying to determine whether he was actually a real teacher. But Tom knew Assistant Warden Overholzer was peering into his soul, searching for guilt.

On his way out of prison that afternoon the black guard, a retired Air Force chief master sergeant, handed Tom an article about how prisoners take advantage of unwitting people.

Was Tom being played? Was the net closing in on him? He wondered in particular when two guards took him to the search room one Thursday as he was coming in to teach.

"Really?" Tom exclaimed when he saw their intent. "Me?"

But he saw right away it was no laughing matter and by the way they searched him that they probably would've found weed in his pen had it been there. They did everything but put on a glove and stick a finger up his ass.

"Nothing personal. Just routine," one of the guards said to him as he was buttoning his shirt.

"Right," Tom said, detecting the smirk in his voice.

"They on to you now," Marcus told him. "You gots to watch your step. You ever heard the term jailhouse snitch? They got a bunch of 'em here; little birds who sing for the warden in the hope she let 'em out of their cage early."

Tom laid low once again and a month went by, so three times a week for four weeks he went through the jail checkpoint clean. That was twelve times. Now Jose and LaRon were really hoping he would run the gauntlet and bring them some weed. Tom thought of this occasionally when he was tending his garden at home, starting seedlings, putting young plants in dirt or cutting down mature ones shining with resin crystals.

What a great hobby. And to put a person in jail for selling, smoking or growing weed? Just plain wrong, Tom reckoned. How he would hate to be in prison unable to grow a few marijuana plants for his PTSD. In fact, the kind of freedom he was fighting for when he served in the armed forces was the kind of freedom that would allow exactly that: a few plants in the basement.

When Tom showed up for class Tuesday, Lieutenant Betcher was waiting for him in the lobby. She sprang to life when she saw him. Current seemed to run through her body.

"You need to come with me," she snapped at Tom.

He followed her down a hallway, heart pounding in his chest.

She stopped at a door, turned the handle and held it open. "After you," she said.

He heard the mockery, though, and the fake sweet sincerity in her voice.

Something was wrong. He could feel it in his bones.

When he walked into the prison conference room, Tom knew he was looking at Warden Jim Jones himself, aka The Warden, a man he had only heard about from his students. What had he heard? That Warden Jones was big and black and had a temper and wasn't by any stretch someone you might say was a kind person. That he started off as a guard forty years ago in the Nebraska penal system, knew all the ins-and-outs and didn't play? Yes, Tom had heard these things and more.

The old prison veteran said nothing. He just stared at Tom, stared at him with the look of a chess master about to take his opponent's king. Furrowed brow, lowered head. Eager eyes.

Assistant Warden Overhozler, sitting next to him, said "Thomas, we'd like to see what's in your bag."

Tom carried a canvas satchel with a shoulder strap. He filled it with books, papers to grade, notes for class, pencils and pens, Kleenex, mints and other such items. "Of course," he said as nonchalantly as possible. But then he paused, playing for time. "Just saying . . . don't you need a search warrant?"

Warden Jones's voice was surprisingly high for a man his size. "Not on federal property we don't. We can search anyone we want."

Lieutenant Betcher swooped in, grabbed his satchel and upended it.

Tom shook his head back and forth disapprovingly as she pawed over the items that tumbled out. Finding nothing, the lieutenant rifled through his books, then the satchel, found nothing and set her sights on his pocket, where a hollowed pen stuffed with two grams of marijuana rested.

"Gimme, gimme," she said, reaching out for him.

He instinctively stepped back. "What the heck!"

Then he heard The Warden's voice: "Don't make me call the guards in and take you down now."

And that was that. They had him. Tom reached in his pocket and tossed the pen on the table. Finding the marijuana inside was no great feat, then, although Lieutenant Betcher acted like it when she popped the cap off and said "Aha!"

Tom was sure that somewhere in Lieutenant Betcher's inner woman, Diana, goddess of the hunt, cheered exultantly at having slain yet another male beast.

Warden Jones chuckled. "Weed in the pen. We seen that one before. Ha ha ha."

And so it turns out Tom did have the right vibe about Ann when she pitched him the job last year. He remembered how she leaned forward and whispered at him, sounding conspiratorial like a palace coup plotter, as if she were letting him in on a secret about teaching in the prison.

Well, a palace coup did occur. It involved Tom. He was deposed from the kingdom of classrooms he ruled and thrown in the dungeon doing five-to-ten in the state penitentiary for smuggling weed in.

And Ann Anderson? Why, Tom heard just the other day she's vice chancellor at the University of Wisconsin!

About The Author

Literary omnivore. Poet. Screenwriter. Short stories. Dreamer. Coffee connoisseur. Vegetarian. Peace advocate. Astronomer. Astrologer. Sun, Ascendant, Venus, Pluto and Mercury in Leo. Animal lover. Reformer. Striving spirit. Raging angel. Grandfather. Military brat. Military veteran. Teacher. Editor. Insomniac. Driven. 100 mph guy in a 50-mph world.

Editor, 6940th Security Wing newspaper,
        Goodfellow AFB, San Angelo, Texas.

Staff Writer, Airman Magazine,
        Kelly AFB, San Antonio, Texas.

Editor, Air Combat Command News Service,
        Langley AFB, Va.

City Hall Reporter,
        The Longview (Texas) News-Journal.

Writing Instructor, English and Business departments, University of Nebraska at Omaha and Metropolitan Community College.

You can reach Craig at
        scriptocanem@thewritingdog.com

Pugh's latest literary works are two volumes of poetry:

A Pocketful of Poems
ISBN 978-0-9701140-3-7

Poems For Pickin'
ISBN 978-0-9701140-1-3

Both are available at your favorite book purveyor upon request, or at Barnes & Noble or Amazon.

Scripto Canem

A Look Back

For all of our friends who bought the original Ganja Tales here's a look back at the line drawings that went with the stories.

REEFER MADNESS

TORCHED

KING CANNABIS

SEE YOU LATER

194

SLINGIN'

SISTERS

BUS BUST

FINDERS KEEPERS

STICKS AND STONES